Cover Copy

He seeks the one his heart desires...

Ailith, the granddaughter of the King of the Fae, travels through time when needed to aid her half-blooded Earthbound kind. Her ability allows her to see visions of war and destruction before it unfolds, and now death is coming for one of the fae warriors she is called to protect, except to save him, she must first discover exactly who he is, and which time he might come from.

Warrior shifter Hunter Matheson is intrigued by Ailith when she arrives through a portal into his twenty-first century time from the year 1211. A feud rages over eight-hundred years in the past between his fae-blooded shifter clan and their neighboring enemy, and now he's driven in his desires for her, would give his life to protect hers. His fierce need for her strikes him deep within. He's certain she's the woman who holds the other half of his soul and now there's nothing he won't do to remain right by her side, no matter what war she seeks to halt, or if he's the very warrior she must save from certain death.

Can Ailith keep Hunter safe, or will he perish exactly as she's foreseen?

Books by Joanne Wadsworth

The Matheson Brothers Series
Highlander's Desire, Book One
Highlander's Passion, Book Two
Highlander's Seduction, Book Three
Highlander's Kiss, Book Four
Highlander's Heart, Book Five
Highlander's Sword, Book Six
Highlander's Bride, Book Seven
Highlander's Caress, Book Eight
Highlander's Touch, Book Nine
Highlander's Shifter, Book Ten
Highlander's Claim, Book Eleven
Highlander's Courage, Book Twelve
Highlander's Mermaid, Book Thirteen

Highlander Heat Series
Highlander's Castle, Book One
Highlander's Magic, Book Two
Highlander's Charm, Book Three
Highlander's Guardian, Book Four
Highlander's Faerie, Book Five
Highlander's Champion, Book Six
Highlander's Captive (Short Story)

Billionaire Bodyguards Series
Billionaire Bodyguard Attraction, Book One
Billionaire Bodyguard Boss, Book Two
Billionaire Bodyguard Fling, Book Three

Books by Joanne Wadsworth

Regency Brides Series

The Duke's Bride, Book One

The Earl's Bride, Book Two

The Wartime Bride, Book Three

The Earl's Secret Bride, Book Four

The Prince's Bride, Book Five

Her Pirate Prince, Book Six

Princesses of Myth Series

Protector, Book One

Warrior, Book Two

Hunter (Short Story - Included in Warrior, Book Two)

Enchanter, Book Three

Healer, Book Four

Chaser, Book Five

Highlander's Claim

The Matheson Brothers, Book Eleven

JOANNE WADSWORTH

Highlander's Claim
ISBN-13: 978-1-99-003441-1
Copyright © 2016, Joanne Wadsworth
Cover Art by Joanne Wadsworth
First electronic publication: July 2017

Joanne Wadsworth
http://www.joannewadsworth.com

AUTHOR'S NOTE:
This book is a work of fiction. The names, characters, places, and incidents are products of the writer's imagination or have been used fictitiously and are not to be construed as real. Any resemblance to persons, living or dead, actual events, locale or organizations is entirely coincidental. The author does not have any control over and does not assume any responsibility for third-party websites or their content.

Published in the United States of America

First digital publication: July 2017
First print publication: July 2017

The Legend

In the twelfth century, a man named Gilleoin became the first and only known man to hold bear shifter blood, an ability gifted to him by The Most High One. His clan was called Matheson, and when he mated with a woman carrying faerie blood, they created a line shrouded in secrecy, a line guarded by the immortal fae princess, Cherub. Through the endless streams of time, she will be there for them, never forsaking her people, either in the present or far into the past.

Cherub –
The Fae Angel of Love and Guardian to her Earthbound Kind

The ancient House of Clan Matheson, led by Gilleoin, the Chief of Matheson, Scotland, 1211, midnight.

Standing on top of the battlements of the castle, Cherub slid her fingers through her warrior mate's as a light breeze blew in over the night-shrouded waters of Loch Alsh. The surface rippled with the reflection of the moon and a glittering array of stars. In the distance, farther along the curve of the bay, the fae village sat, the homes cloistered tightly together and surrounded by a tall stone wall. Puffs of smoke escaped the thatched-roof abodes and sparks flared from the central fire pit. Cherub leaned her cheek against Kirk's shoulder and softly sighed. "I wish there was more I could do to bring those of my fae kind who are soul-bound together. I'm always anxiously awaiting the next full moon to rise, for the air itself to bring to me the secrets it holds."

"Then we wait, and while we do, we keep an eye on our enemy." Kirk brought her hand to his mouth and gently kissed her fingertips, his lips whisper-soft and his touch warming her heart and soul. As he turned his gaze back out over the water, he surveyed their enemy's war galley with its taut sail out at sea. The Chief of MacKenzie's crest flapped from the center mast, Colin MacKenzie himself captaining his vessel from the bow.

Their warring enemy was a thorn in their side, a ruthless chief and warrior determined on staking his claim both on their Matheson land here at the tip of Loch Alsh, and their half fae-blooded people within the village along the loch. MacKenzie was ruthless, a man who fought to the death to take what he wanted, and they'd come up against him time and time again over the years. He was a deadly threat, but she and Kirk, along with her three nieces who'd offered their aid, would turn the tide of this war in their favor. Even now her nieces remained at the warrior encampment farther along their land to the east, where their land bordered Colin MacKenzie's. Ailith, Cairstine, and Lilias would never falter in their duty of ensuring their Matheson kin continued to hold this land, but most of all, they wouldn't falter in protecting those of their fae blooded kind who lived here on Earth.

Kirk raised a leather gauntleted hand to the guardsman on duty in the gatehouse and called out, "Alert the point watchman to maintain a vigilant eye while our enemy sails these waters."

The guardsman lifted his horn and blew. One long blast echoed out over the water and once the MacKenzie had sailed around the corner, an answering trumpeted blast carried to them on the breeze from the point watchman. One blast only, which meant the MacKenzie had continued toward his own stronghold where Loch Alsh met Loch Long.

Cherub blew out a long breath and relaxed into Kirk's side as he wrapped his arm around her. "We are always on tenterhooks where Colin MacKenzie is concerned. I wish we could be done with him, once and for all."

"I wish for the same, but thankfully we've won each battle

he's instigated thus far and we'll continue to do so. We're Mathesons and we'll fight until we no longer can."

"I wholeheartedly—" Three elusive golden threads suddenly swirled all about and she stretched her fingertips toward them. They fluttered all around her hands, threads belonging to her three nieces. She'd never mistake them, not when her nieces were tied to her very essence through their deep family bond.

"Do you see something?" Kirk searched her gaze. "Is something wrong?"

"Nay, but I can see Ailith, Cairstine, and Lilias's essences, three beautiful golden tendrils." Her nieces were the beloved daughters of her brother, Cian, the greatest healer amongst their people beyond the veil. Her nieces had also been awaiting their chosen ones these past eight-hundred years, but no bond had yet taken ahold for them with another of their full-blooded fae kind.

Arms raised, she searched out farther with her fae senses as the wind rose and rushed all about. As an immortal time-walker and the faerie king's daughter, 'twas her duty to see any soul bound matches made, and she did so by opening portals in time and bringing together those who were mated, no matter how many centuries separated them.

With her regal red skirts brushing her ankles, she lifted free from the stony walkway of the ramparts and breezed higher. She swished through the air, her long draping satin sleeves brushing over the backs of her hands as she settled down gently within the closest crenellation.

Kirk bounded up behind her onto the thin ledge, wrapped him arms tight around her middle and held her close, his shifter body a wicked wall of heat at her back and his forearms rippling with fur below the rolled cuffs of his tunic. With his leather-clad legs braced wide apart and his dark hair brushing his shoulders, he was every inch her warrior protector. "Don't let me disturb you," he murmured. "Seek the knowledge you're after."

"I need to see where their essences are drawn to." She swished her hands through the air and the three golden threads belonging to her nieces whisked away on the wind toward another place in time, Murdock's time. "Oh my, they're being drawn to your twenty-first century, Kirk. I'm certain of it."

"Interesting." Kirk licked her neck and nipped her throbbing pulse point.

"It has been three years since I last took my nieces to visit Murdock, but I clearly need to again." Her eldest niece's essence whipped ahead of her sisters' essences and disappeared first into the glittering array of the stars. Excited, she bounced around and wrapped her arms around Kirk's neck. "Aye, my beloved nieces are certainly next. I need to discover who they're soul bound to."

"You can't sense who they're mated to yet?"

"Nay, I cannae tell, but I shall once the next full moon rises, when the men they're mated to will be driven to begin the hunt of their chosen one."

"Then it sounds like we have another mission ahead of us. I've actually been silently hoping your nieces would be next. They're so courageous, strong, and fiercely independent. They'll be a good match for any of my clansmen from my own time, likely run them ragged too, just as their aunt did with me." Pressing her back against the edge of the crenellation, he trapped her between him and the craggy stone. With his hands sliding around her upper torso, he brushed his thumbs along the undersides of her breasts, and made them ache in a delicious way.

"I love it when you touch me like this."

"I believe I love it more." He cupped her full breasts in his hands and the ache intensified. Heat coiled low in her belly and flared out. Oh my, she needed even more of his divine touch. "Cloak us, Cherub. I intend on having my wicked way with you right now. Say aye."

"Aye." With a mere thought from her mind alone, she

cloaked their forms and lifted them free of the ramparts and sent them soaring skyward, right over the loch where the stars twinkled the brightest. She caught her mate's mouth and kissed him with all the love and devotion she held deep inside her, and he kissed her back just as ravenously.

High enough now that they couldn't be seen by anyone below, she uncloaked their forms and stroked her fingers along his stubbly jaw. His beautiful golden shifter gaze devoured hers, his mind tunneling deep inside her own mind along their merged link, one he'd created the night they'd first joined together, a link inherent in his shifter line.

"*You are my everything, Kirk,*" she whispered to him.

"*I couldn't survive without you. You are the light of my life, the woman I live for, love without question, and wish to hold close for the rest of our lives.*" He tipped her back in his arms and as he did, she swept them higher and higher toward the heavens, giving herself completely over to the depth of their bond and the intense love they held for each other.

This was the soul bond.

This was what she wanted for all her fae kind.

This was eternal love.

Chapter 1

The Matheson warrior encampment, the next night…

Wispy streaks of fog clung to the still surface of Loch Alsh along the pebbly shoreline of their Matheson land edging their warrior encampment. Not a ripple marred the surface, the darkened waters holding the mirrored image of the sliver of moon high above and a smattering of glittering stars. Ailith thumbed her chin as she eyed Cherub and Kirk, who seemed to have strange smiles on their faces tonight, like they did when they knew something she didn't. "Are you two going to spill the beans? What's causing those smiles?"

"We're smiling?" Still smiling, but now covertly, Cherub leaned back against Kirk and her mate encircled his arms around her waist, his chin resting on the top of her aunt's golden head.

Witnessing the intense love which flowed between her aunt and Kirk always brought such a sense of wonder to her very soul. Cherub had been alone for a thousand years before finally finding her chosen one, and oh, what a journey her aunt had experienced when Kirk had begun his chase of her. Never had her aunt imagined she'd be able to continue doing to duty while mated to her warrior shifter, but Kirk had given Cherub his vow to always remain at her side and offer her his aid, and hadn't faltered. She and her sisters had stepped up too, helping to ease the burden by remaining here at their warrior encampment. "We share everything with each other. You must spill."

"Well, what if I told you that last night I sensed yours and your sisters' essences forming a soul bond with men from the twenty-first century, within Murdock Matheson's clan?"

"Please, dinnae say you're pulling my leg." She and her sisters had remained unmated for centuries upon centuries, and they'd all but given up the hope that they'd ever forge a mated bond with another. 'Twas what they desired though, with all their hearts.

"No leg pulling, I promise." Cherub crossed her heart. "I'm not exactly aware of who the three of you are mated to, but I certainly saw your essence and your sisters' being pulled through time. Yours soared through first, quickly followed by Cairstine's then Lilias's."

"'Tis another three weeks until the full moon rises, and we both know it takes a full moon for you to sense any mated bond actually taking form between a mated pair." How irritating. She had a mate awaiting her in another time, only she would have to wait three weeks before the chase could begin.

"Aye, that is true, but 'tis only a matter of time now until we discover who you're mated to. Those three weeks will pass in a blink of time. I'm certain of it."

"Whenever my sisters or I have traveled to the twenty-first century, you've never allowed anyone other than Murdock, the Chief of Matheson, to see us. Will that change?"

"Aye, of course. You would be permitted to show yourself to all within Murdock's clan now." Cherub settled a hand on her shoulder, her gown's rich ruby skirts embellished with white lace swishing in the gentle breeze. "If you wish to go sooner rather than later, I will gladly take you. 'Twill give you a chance to meet Murdock's kinsmen and get to know them afore the full moon rises."

"I'm needed here at the warrior encampment at present, to be alert for any visions." One had struck her yesterday, but the images had remained too grainy to decipher. The vision should return soon though, stronger and without any issue. When it did, she would discover exactly what she needed to do to protect her kin here at the encampment. Lowering to a crouch in her black leather breeches and loose-sleeved cream tunic, her wrist daggers sheathed and sword belted at her side, she gently laid one palm against the land. This was how she connected to her visions, by touching the soil beneath her feet.

A gentle hum emanated from the fae who lived at the village farther along the loch, the sweet cadence one that spoke to her very heart. Searching farther afield with her combat skill, she followed the curve of the land for several miles until she reached Colin MacKenzie's stronghold. She sent her senses down deeper and hit an oily residue, one which blackened her vision. Pushing past it, she sought more.

Images swirled, a barrage rolling one over top of the other and she clutched ahold of the strongest of the images and locked it in place. No graininess. Far better than yesterday. Exactly what she was after. Colin MacKenzie stormed along a darkened passageway deep within the lower bowels of the earth, his fists clenched and the two war braids plaited in his shaggy brown hair swaying. He rounded a corner and stepped up to a guardsman on duty, the dank and musty recesses of the passageway clogging the air and her throat. Keeping her focus though, she stayed with the MacKenzie as he snatched a ring of keys from the guard, selected the right one and slotted it into the lock of a thick cell door with panels of steel. These were his dungeons, of which she and Cherub had never been able to trace the exact location of, an annoyance for certain, although one day they would find them.

Metal scraped against the stone and dirt floor and the MacKenzie swung the door open and stepped inside. She followed him and entered a cell which reeked of blood and death. A single candle, almost burnt to the wick in an iron holder in the corner, cast its flickering glow over the blackened stone walls, and in one corner, a man hung from the ceiling, his wrists clamped and chained high, his body caked in dirt from head to toe. Only the whites of his eyes showed as he narrowed them on the helmed guardsman exacting his torture. The guardsman slammed his fists into the captive's side, then swung him about on the chains and landed more punches into his back. Brutal hit after hit landed, and the prisoner's pained grunts echoed within the cell and squeezed at her very heart. He got wrenched about, his tunic and breeches torn into shreds.

"Stand aside," MacKenzie issued to his torturer and the brutal beast came to attention, his beady black eyes staring back from behind the slit in his helm. With a nod, MacKenzie gripped the prisoner's sides, gave a shove and sent him slamming back into the wall. The warrior lifted his head and roared, kicked free of the wall and the spikes he'd been impaled on and swung forward. Blood oozed down his back, flowing over the shredded bits of his tunic, his blood dripping into a pool of rusty-red at his feet.

MacKenzie sauntered around to the prisoner's back and eyed the bloodied spike holes. "Hmm, interesting. You are the first Matheson warrior who has survived more than an hour with my torturer. What possibly keeps you alive? Could it be the lass you guarded with your life at the warrior encampment during our battle?"

The warrior gritted his teeth, but uttered not a word.

Scowling, MacKenzie stepped back around in front of the prisoner. "I've admired the lass for a long time, her ability to move amongst Gilleoin's warriors, as one with them as any man would be. She has two sisters as well, but I'm after the one who is lethal with her blade and can hit a target with her bow and arrow from over a hundred feet distant. I'm certain she's one of the full-blooded fae and that makes her a treasure to capture and make mine. You should never have boarded my galley in your attempt to save her life. You only ensured your own death when you did."

"Leave Ailith alone." The ragged demand escaped the prisoner's lips, and she gasped. He knew her name?

Colin MacKenzie pulled back his fist and swung.

Thump. Thump. Thump.

Claws sliced free of the warrior's fingers and fur rippled across his body then just as swiftly retracted. A warrior shifter. She didn't recognize him. He certainly wasn't Gilleoin or either of his two sons, nor was he Kirk. How did he know her?

"Well, well. I wondered if you were of shifter blood since you're still alive." MacKenzie let off an evil laugh. "You're clearly a 'son of Gilleoin,' although you are neither his firstborn or second-born from his fae wife, and there are only two heirs. So," he muttered, the evil glimmer in his eyes flickering. "Where did you come from and by what name are you known?"

"I am from a place and time you could never imagine." The warrior's eyes blazed a rich golden shifter hue, a gaze full of deadly intent. Hers likely blazed with the same intent too. She itched to wrap her fingers around Colin MacKenzie's neck. A quick twist and she'd be done with him. Hurting her kin wasn't permitted.

"Tell me, and I shall offer you your life in return."

"I would sooner have you slice my head from my shoulders than ever speak to you again."

"Then I shall oblige." MacKenzie slid his sword free and pressed it against the warrior's throat. Leaning into his ear, he muttered, "Can a shifter survive the loss of his head?"

"What we can't survive is the loss of our chosen one, and I promise you, Ailith is mine."

"Nay, she is mine. I shall speak vows with her, and soon she will carry my son and when she does, I'll have ensured the strongest fae blood runs directly through my line."

"Ailith will never consent to being your wife. Touch her and I'll kill you." The prisoner lifted his head and roared, and as he did, the MacKenzie sank his blade even deeper into his neck. Blood spurted, so much blood, too much blood.

It coated her vision and she jerked back, her hand trembling on the pebbly shoreline, the moon aglow high overhead. Tears streamed down her cheeks and she couldn't halt her sobs. The warrior was about to lose his life and even though she didn't know him, had never met him, she clearly would meet him soon. From her vision, he'd certainly known her.

"Tell me what you saw, Ailith." Cherub crouched before her, her aunt's skin sparkling in the moonlight and giving evidence of the fact she was their fae king's firstborn.

"I saw a son of Gilleoin being brutally beaten after his capture at Colin MacKenzie's hand, although he wasnae Kenneth or Ivan, Gilleoin's sons. He told the Chief of MacKenzie he was my mate, although he was unrecognizable, caked in dirt and restrained deep in MacKenzie's dungeons." Still trembling, she gripped the pouch of faerie dust swaying at her hip. "I need to find this warrior shifter who believes we're mated and see if what he says is true. Then, I must ensure he can never travel to this time. My vision proves he is the one I need to protect next from the MacKenzie's murderous hand."

"Then we'll leave, this very moment, for Murdock's time. I have no issue going now." Cherub swirled her fingers through the air and the wind rose and whipped all about. A portal opened and her aunt grasped her hand as a powerful blast of air swirled. Kirk gripped Cherub's waist from behind and the three of them fell away into the dark, churning abyss.

Stars sparkled and lightning flashed. Ailith's heartbeat pounded and sheer exhilaration raced through her, just as it always did when she traveled so swiftly through time and space. Over the wild wind, she yelled, "The warrior's face might have been unrecognizable, but I got a good sense of his height, build, and voice. I'd surely know him if I met him." Or at least she hoped she would. She had to ensure he never had the chance to travel to the past and perish because of her.

"Let's hope you find him swiftly." Cherub twirled her fingers again and the wind slowed and the darkness receded. "We're about to land."

Ailith bumped down onto solid ground, right within the inner sanctum of Murdock's solar. With the whistling wind still churning, papers scattered across the desk, a pen clattered to the floor and the navy drapes either side of the window swayed. Slowly, the air calmed and she let go of her aunt's arm. "We need to find Murdock."

"I'll scout him out, while you two remain here." Kirk squeezed Ailith's shoulder. "That'll give you some time to analyze your vision, and the fact you're allowed to show yourself to everyone here. It'll be a big adjustment."

"Thank you." She wouldn't mind some time to adjust.

"He pressed a kiss to the top of Cherub's head. "I won't be long, my love."

"We'll stay here for the night, and for as long as Ailith needs us to remain until she uncovers who it is she needs to protect." Her aunt tweaked Kirk's nose. "And dinnae find any trouble while you're scouting. When you say *my love,* all sweet and innocent like that, 'tis a clear indication you intend to."

"Nothing ever escapes your notice." Grinning, Kirk breathed deep and lifted his nose. His jaw fell open on a moan. "Mmm, I can already scent cinnamon sugar donuts. Hell, I've missed being back in my own time. There's a stash of chocolate in the kitchens here too, damn good chocolate. I'll bring you two some when I return."

"You'd better, and oh, dinnae forget, I'm rather partial to Cadbury milk chocolate, with caramel inside, if that's within the stash." Cherub smiled sweetly at him.

"Righto. Donuts and caramel chocolate coming right up." Kirk gripped the hilt of his sword as he strode to the door, halted in the doorway and nodded resolutely over his shoulder. "Ladies, this is an incredibly important mission, and I won't let anyone stand in my way of the donuts or chocolate. I promise you both I shall return with them."

Ailith barely suppressed her laugh. Her aunt and Kirk always knew how to lighten the mood at just the right time, particularly when pressure pressed down on her. With her combat skill, an element of pressure always existed and right now even more so, particularly when she had a warrior to find and keep safe. A warrior who might just be her mate.

"Kirk, dinnae forget to bring Murdock too." Cherub pinched his backside.

"That's right. Murdock." Kirk wagged a finger at Cherub then disappeared out the door. "I won't forget," he called back, his voice echoing to them. "Whatever you ask, will be provided."

"He is such a delight." Still smiling, Cherub crossed to the window. She stood there, peering out over the inner courtyard, then slowly, her expression changed. She worriedly nibbled on her lower lip. "A warrior's life lays in the balance, and we must discover exactly who he is."

"Aye, we must." She rolled her shoulders, gave them a quick shake up and down and tried to relax, although tension coiled deep in her gut. She fisted one hand over her pouch of fae dust swinging from her hip. Usually, once Cherub brought her here, her aunt either extended her cloaking over her, or she herself sprinkled a little fae dust and made a wish to remain unseen. Either worked rather well. No dust was needed right now though. She would finally be able to meet Murdock's clansmen, in the flesh.

She walked past the forest-green couch tucked along one wall and halted before the stunning black and white framed drawing of Matheson Castle as it had stood over eight-hundred years ago. Her mate might not be from the past where she'd spent a great deal of time of late at the warrior encampment, but he was here, in this time. Staggering. It hadn't yet fully sunk in.

"Come here, Ailith." Cherub opened the window and beckoned her over with a wave of her hand. "Send your senses out. See if you can see anything new now we're here in the same time as the warrior."

"Of course, I should have done so already." Usually she needed to connect to the soil itself for a vision, but if one were close to rising and she caught the sensation of it, she could whip outside, plant her hand on the ground and connect more fully so those images would strengthen. She trotted around Murdock's chunky wooden desk and joined Cherub at the window. Moonlight peppered through the thick darkened clouds overhead, while below in the inner courtyard all appeared calm and quiet. "'Tis late. Everyone is abed."

"Nay, this castle never sleeps. There are plenty of guards on duty. See, right there." Cherub pointed across to the other side of the inner bailey.

A warrior strode out of the gatehouse and walked along the battlements. He halted at the corner crenellation and crossed his wide forearms on the craggy stone edge, his shoulders wide as he peered into the darkened depths of the forest beyond. Clouds parted and the moon lit the white of the warrior's shirt a soft golden color. His Matheson plaid was hooked around his waist with a leather belt and the burnished hilt of his claymore glinted at his hip. Aye, the warriors of this time still adhered to the old ways, their shifter blood running far hotter than most and their need to expend their great energy ensuring they trained daily with the sword. She dug her fingers into the stone windowsill and closed her eyes. She breathed the fresh night air deep into her lungs and waited. No images came forth, so she opened her eyes and shook her head at Cherub. "There is naught yet."

"Still, you should remain alert. A vision willnae be far away."

"I shall." She cleared her throat, nodded at the warrior who'd drawn her attention. "Who's that guardsman across the way?"

"Hunter Matheson."

"Is he one of the unmated warriors?"

"Aye, and has been these past six years." Cherub's brows pinched together. "Does he draw your interest for some reason?"

"Nay, he's only the first warrior I've seen." Yet for some reason he had drawn her interest. His dark hair was cropped close to his head, no more than an inch or two long, with a wayward lock curling across his forehead. Her fingers tingled with the need to sweep that errant lock back and oh my, he had two sweet dimples either side of his lips. How adorable.

"You need to meet each and every one of the thirty-six unmated men here, and as quickly as possible." Cherub clasped her shoulder and squeezed. "Do you think you can identify the warrior who insisted you were mated from just his voice alone?"

"Hopefully, aye."

"I might be able to help you with that identification as well." Murdock Matheson, the seer and chief of this clan, trod into the chamber wearing a dark blue button-down shirt and gray dress pants, his brown hair wisped with a little silver at the sides.

Kirk brought up the rear with a plate brimming with donuts and chunks of caramel chocolate piled on it. He grinned as if he'd won the lottery, then held out the plate with a flourish of one hand to her and Cherub. "Never say I don't deliver, my ladies."

"You always deliver, my tempting bear." Cherub pinched a donut and some chocolate and bit into a mouthful of each. Moaning, she eyed Murdock. "That's good, but down to business. How might you be able to help with that identification, my dear friend?"

"I caught the same vision as Ailith did." Murdock plucked a donut from the plate and handed it to Ailith.

"Thank you." She accepted it and chewed. Oooh, de-licious. The flavors of the cinnamon and sugar danced across her tongue. Once she'd finished her mouthful, she continued, "So, you're saying you saw the same vision as I did, of the warrior imprisoned within MacKenzie's cells and his conversation with MacKenzie?"

"Aye, and I'll never allow one of my own men to be beheaded at that monster's hand."

"Neither will I." She would stand by that vow. "Who is the warrior?"

"His voice was raspy and rough, but from what I sensed at the time, including his build and height, he can be one of only three men. Hunter, one of my best trackers, Liam who's our resident clan doctor, or possibly Levi who holds the skill of apport."

Apport was a skill greatly admired by many of her kind beyond the veil, one in which that person could make solid objects materialize out of thin air. She shook her head. "Surely if Levi was the warrior within my vision, then he could have brought forth a tool into the dungeons to cut through his chains, correct?"

"I considered that, but if there is a great deal of steel lining the cell door, it can play havoc with his ability. He may not have been able to apport what he needed into the cell to free himself."

"No' even the keys from the guardsman?"

"Not even that." A frustrated shake of his head.

"I see, then I wish to speak to all three men, this very night if I might."

"There's more." Murdock bit into a donut from the plate too, his expression thoughtful. "What I don't understand from the vision, is why the warrior claimed you two were mated, when it's impossible to know until the full moon rises. That's still three weeks away, and this vision is current. What we've seen will happen within the next few days, that's if the warrior leaves with you once you discover who he is."

"I thought the same following my vision, although he might just be saying what he believes to be the truth, even though that truth is yet to be uncovered. No matter what though, once I've discovered who he might be, then I'll ensure he remains right here in this time while I return to the past." She eyed her aunt as Cherub sucked madly on a chunk of chocolate. "Do you agree with this plan?"

"I completely agree," Cherub mumbled around her mouthful before popping another chunk between her lips. "This chocolate is divine. You haven't had some yet."

"I'm pacing myself." She ate the last bite of her donut, then helped herself to a chunk of chocolate and nearly melted at the rich, silky smooth texture which glided down her throat as she sucked on it. "I should travel here more often."

"You should." Murdock chuckled, then eyed Cherub. "There's more of that chocolate in the dresser drawer of your chamber. I dropped it in there myself after I caught sight of your coming arrival."

"Seers are the best, which is why I love visiting you." Cherub popped a kiss on Murdock's cheek then grasped Ailith's hands. "I'm going to leave you to speak to the three warriors on your own. Take some time to speak to each one individually. Soak in their voices and identify the warrior we need to protect."

"Aye, I surely will."

"My chamber is three doors down on the right, so should you need me, come and knock."

"I will. Sleep well." She hugged her aunt, and Cherub swept one hand through the crook in Kirk's elbow and steered him out the door with the remainder of the delicious offerings on the plate still in his hand.

"Come with me." Murdock gestured for her to follow him.

"I've a chamber you can use for the night too, which I'll show you now so you can retire to it whenever you please during the night."

"Thank you. That would be lovely." At his side, she wandered down the wooden paneled hallway, the thick blue and green woolen runner underneath her feet lining the center of the passageway. Darkened wooden doors led off each side, while overhead light streamed from the recessed lights tucked into the ceiling. Modern technology. How wonderful it was.

At the end of the passageway, Murdock halted before the last door and pushed it open. He motioned for her to go in first and she stepped past him into one of his guest chambers. A large bed sat against one wall, covered in a burgundy and white tartan quilt with plush white pillows propped against the chestnut headboard. Along another wall sat a matching chestnut dresser with an elaborately designed and framed looking glass.

"This guest chamber shares a bathroom with the connecting chamber next door." Murdock crossed the room and opened the top dresser drawer. "There's chocolate in here for you too, along with nightwear and a dressing robe. "I'll ask Isla to bring some more clothes by in the morning. She'll have plenty you can choose from."

"Thank you, and hopefully I can discover who this warrior is afore the morning and I can be away as soon as possible." She opened the bathroom door, which had another door on the other side. The marble vanity countertop gleamed, as did the glass sides of the shower cubicle. Perfect. All she needed was right here. "Who resides in the connecting chamber?"

"It's usually allocated for guests, except Hunter is currently occupying the room since his chamber is undergoing a renovation. Come with me. We'll go and find the men you seek. The sooner you meet them all, the better." Murdock caught her elbow and guided her back down the passageway to the stairs leading to the lower floor.

Eager, she bounded downstairs ahead of him, her tension draining away. A little excitement even swarmed through her. She'd finally be able to show herself to Murdock's clansmen and naught more could have pleased her. In the foyer, wide double doors engraved with the Matheson clan crest stood open and she walked into the great hall filled with trestle tables and a roaring fireplace to the side. Blue suede couches curved around the fire blazing in the hearth and a warrior lay stretched out on one of the couches, his navy pants encasing long legs and his ankle dagger glinting where he'd crossed his feet and the hem had lifted. Firelight played over his chiseled features, his dark hair clearly the same length and cut as the warrior from her vision. Right height and build as the prisoner too. She definitely needed to speak to him.

"That's Levi," Murdock whispered in her ear before crossing to the man and nudging his arm. "Up you get, sleepyhead."

One long groan, his eyes still closed. "Hunter, I'm not supposed to take over from you for another half an hour. Go away."

"I'm not Hunter." Murdock rustled Levi's hair.

"Chief?" Levi cranked one eye open and groaned again, then toppled from the couch as he caught sight of her. "Who do we have here?" Quick as a whip, he bounded to his feet, then slowly sauntered across to her before pulling her into a back-breaking hug she hadn't expected. She gasped and got a mouthful of his cotton shirtfront as she tried to speak. "Mmm," he rumbled in her ear. "I scent unmated female. Give me your name, sweet pea."

"Levi, meet Ailith." Murdock motioned to her. "She's one of the full-blooded fae, the daughter of Cian, the prince and healer of our fae kind beyond the veil, and the niece of Cherub. Ailith, meet Levi, one of my senior officers who is desperate to find his mate. He can be a terrible flirt too. Just warning you."

"Thank you for the delightful welcome, Levi." She managed to tip her head back and get some much-needed air, except she came eye to eye with him as she did.

"Anytime." Another rumbling answer as he kept his gaze on hers while asking Murdock, "Chief, can I keep her?"

"Not unless she's your mate." The chief chuckled. "Ailith holds the skill of combat sense and can receive visions of war before they unfold. She's foreseen the death of a warrior from our time who perishes far in the past, and now she's here to discover exactly who he is so she can ensure his protection, a warrior who spoke of being mated to her." Murdock thumped Levi on the back. "Don't break her bones, son. She doesn't hold the strength of a shifter."

"I'm sorry. You're not hurt, are you?" Levi released her, so swiftly, worry flashing across his face.

She tumbled back into another man. 'Twas Hunter, the warrior she'd watched from the chief's solar window. She cleared her throat, righted herself and stepped back from him. His golden shifter eyes blazed a molten hue, the same shade as that of the prisoner she needed to find and protect. Unfortunately, 'twas also the same shade that everyone held within this clan, a true indicator of their shifter blood.

Hunter's gaze narrowed, his eyebrows pinching together. "I caught the chief's introduction. Who is this warrior you're looking for?"

"I'm unaware of his name, and all I caught in my vision was the sound of his voice. He was caked in dirt from head to foot, as if he'd been wallowing in mud, then hung from chains in the MacKenzie's dungeons and tortured before having his throat slit. 'Twas a rather gruesome death to witness."

"It definitely sounds it."

"I'm here to ensure that warrior's protection, to keep him alive." She thumbed her chin as his voice washed over her. It could be a match, although so too could Levi's. Gosh, how annoying. She'd hoped the warrior's voice would be instantly recognizable, that she'd know beyond a shadow of a doubt exactly who had featured in her vision. "Ah, your chief saw the same vision as I did and believes either you, Liam, or Levi are a match to the warrior who perishes. I need to meet Liam too, so I can listen to all three of you speaking and see if I can uncover which one of you is about to perish."

"I'm Liam." Another warrior leaned against the doorway wearing a white collared lab coat flapping over pressed beige pants and polished boots. A pen was hooked in his front coat pocket and a small pad poked out of his pants pocket.

"You're the resident doctor?"

"Aye, and I could scent you from the other side of the keep." He stalked toward her, halted in front and crossed his large arms across an equally large chest. "You smell damn good, like an unmated female. Are you?"

"I too scented her, from outside on the ramparts." Scowling, Hunter stepped away toward the narrow window overlooking the inner courtyard, the stained glass sparkling with deep reds, blues, and greens. With his forehead pressed against the glass, his shoulders shook as a low growl rumbled from deep within his chest.

"Are you all right?" She took one tentative step toward him.

"Aye, I'm fine." Hand shoved up, Hunter canted his head in a very animal-like way. "Stay right where you are. You don't only smell like an unmated female, but you're also in heat and the fragrance you're emitting has just gotten a whole lot sweeter and more lethal."

"You must be wrong. I cannae be in heat." As an immortal, she'd never physically aged past her twentieth year and due to her immortality, her courses fell a good twenty or so years apart. She wasn't due for another flow for years yet."

"I'm not wrong. You're in heat."

She lifted a brow at Murdock, who surely would have

scented such a thing and warned her by now. "Can you scent I'm in heat?"

"You weren't in heat on your arrival, but something's changed since we entered the great hall." Murdock stuck his hands in his pockets and pursed his lips. "I'd have to agree with my men. You're in the early stages of being in heat."

"'Tis too soon, and I am never early."

"I agree with Hunter and Liam." Levi lifted his nose to the air and breathed deep with a mischievous smile. "You're definitely in heat, sweet pea, and your scent has been gaining in strength while we've been standing here chatting."

"Then 'tis best I get down to the business at hand." Three unmated males stood in this room, and each one followed her every move with their acute shifter gazes as she walked back and forth between them. She took in their size and build, the way they held themselves and their mannerisms. All were so very similar, which meant discovering which man was the one she needed to save would be more difficult to uncover than she'd first believed. Even their voices as yet hadn't given the one she sought away.

She halted beside Hunter first, gently laid her hand over one of his clenched fists on the windowsill. "You seem to be the most affected by my presence."

"I like how you smell, and so does my bear. He can be quite territorial, particularly around unmated females. That's because I've had a younger sister to protect until this past month when she accepted the bond with her mate."

"What's her name?"

"Bella. She an empath and a fierce little shifter."

An image of Bella flittered through her mind, her sweet empath nature strong, her inner bear definitely a fierce little fighter. It had been three years since her last visit here to Murdock's time, and even though she hadn't uncloaked herself to Bella when she'd caught sight of her arguing with Jamie one day in the courtyard, she'd still known exactly who she and Jamie were. Bella and Jamie had been beyond the veil in spiritual form for centuries as they'd both awaited their rebirth to occur here in this time, although both of them had been reborn as babes, and as such had no memories of their past and all that had occurred. That was the way for the odd couple who required rebirth, particularly when they were taken far too young from this world and hadn't been given the chance to complete their bond with their mate. "I spent time with Bella beyond the veil. Your sister was a delight to be around, although rather prone to getting into others' business, even in her spiritual form, but that is simply because of her fae empath ability."

"Empaths are nosy. They can't help it."

"I would love to see her while I'm here."

"She and Jamie are currently away on their honeymoon."

"Oh, then I shall catch up with them both on their return." She would look forward to it. She cleared her throat and returned her thoughts to her mission at hand. "Hmm, I thought I'd be able to identify the warrior from my vision, from your voices, only I still cannae say which one of you he might be. Mayhap if I spoke to you all privately, I'll get more of a sense of which warrior it is I need to protect." As it was, all she could sense was their growing frustration with her overpowering scent, which was only adding to her own frustration too. How annoying she was in heat. If only that hadn't happened until it should have.

Still, she'd deal with her scent right now, remove it from this great hall then get back to doing her job.

From her pouch, she wriggled two fingers inside, pinched a little golden dust and tossed it high over the men. "With this fae dust," she chanted, "allow my scent to lift from this great hall. Draw it higher and disperse it."

She settled back on her heels and took in each of the three men.

They snorted under their breath and prowled in a circle

around her, mayhap even more tense than before. "Is, ah, all well?"

"You shouldn't have spelled your scent away." Hunter leaned in, his nose in her hair as he breathed deep. "You smell wrong now, as if you're hiding an important part of who you are. Bring your scent back."

"Wait." Liam gripped Hunter's shoulder. "I believe she was right to spell her scent from this hall tonight. Our focus needs to be on her vision right now, on discovering who she needs to protect, so that we can protect her in return."

"And which one of us might be mated to her while she makes that discovery." Levi cracked his knuckles. "I for one want to find out before the next full moon rises. Three weeks is a lifetime away. If she's mine, then I want her now."

"Excuse me," she interrupted and pushed the men back from her. "I would have you know I am a highly trained warrior. I dinnae carry a sword for no reason. I can certainly look after myself. I'm here to protect you, no' the other way around."

"Well said." Levi pulled her into another smothering hug and squeezed her tight. "But you're still a woman and make no mistake, we've been brought up to protect our women at all costs. They are the future of our clan, and only through them can we ensure our kind don't fall into extinction."

"I understand, but—"

"Let her go, Levi." Hunter grasped Levi's shoulder. "Your scent is all over her and my bear doesn't like it."

"Cease fighting." She squirmed out of Levi's hold and grasped Hunter's muscled bicep. "I'll begin by getting to know you first, Hunter." She smiled at Liam and Levi. "'Tis time for me to begin my work here. I'll speak to you two later, mayhap in the morning since Levi is due on duty, taking over from Hunter if I caught Murdock and Levi's conversation right earlier."

"You did." Murdock nodded his agreement.

"We'll definitely speak in the morning." Levi sent her a

teasing wink and blew her a kiss. "Breakfast is on me, here in the great hall. I'll save a seat for you. Do you like bacon and eggs?"

"Quit it, Romeo." Liam smacked Levi in the arm then eyed her. "He's the tease around here, in case you missed that. I'll catch up with you in the morning too. No need to track me down again tonight."

"Wonderful." She dipped her head at each man, including Murdock. "Please, keep me informed if you have any further visions. I see a great deal afore war looms, but I dinnae always see all, no' as a seer can."

"Of course." Murdock slapped Hunter on the back. "I've given Ailith the guest chamber next to yours. Ensure she returns to it without any issue."

"I'll guard her with my life." Hunter curled his hand over hers on his arm, then led her through the double doors into the dark of the night.

Outside, torches mounted along the curtain wall sent soft golden light flickering over the night-shrouded courtyard and up high over the battlements above. She strolled at Hunter's side, along the cobbled pathway leading around the perimeter of the bailey toward the postern gate.

As they passed under the stone arch, the wind rose and swirled all around her, while up on top of the corner crenellation, a camera mounted on the stone whirred as it slowly moved to take in the wide expanse of the forest. "Your twenty-first century surveillance technology is quite remarkable."

"What's more remarkable is how you know my younger sister." He led her down the grassy trail and into the shadowed depths of the pine trees where the camera could no longer reach them. "That surprised me."

"Over the centuries, I've come to know many of our fae kind. You though, I know very little about." She traversed the winding trail down toward the pebbly foreshore, then halted on the grassy bank and smiled as she took in the long length of the inner channel of Loch Alsh. Home. No matter what century she traveled to, this was always home. The waters shimmered a midnight-black and reflected the moon's glow across its rippled surface. "This land has no' changed in all these centuries. 'Tis always a wonder to behold."

"The fae village has certainly changed." Hunter eased in behind her, his big body providing solid protection and an undeniable element of heat, which sent tingles racing through her body. She rarely allowed any man to stand at her back, but this felt right, strangely right. In her ear, he continued, "Unfortunately, it fell into disrepair centuries ago, but we've managed to rebuild one of the homes and we're going to start on the second later this month."

"That is wonderful news." With one hand raised to her brow, she searched the shoreline leading around the curve of the bay to the point. Moonlight played over the thatched roof of one home standing all alone within the crumbled remains of the outer stone wall. Gently, she swayed back against Hunter, until her back fully rested on his chest. She wriggled against him and he swept one arm around her waist and pinned her close. Oh my, the tingles returned and tightened her nipples. "I w-would love to see it."

"I'll take you tomorrow. I promise you I shall."

"I'll take you up on that kind offer, should I still be here."

"You truly only wish to discover who the warrior is, then leave?"

"Aye, his protection comes afore all else, and should he travel to the past then that is where he shall ultimately perish, and should we be soul bound, then what kind of a mate would I be to allow his death when I know I can halt it?" Which meant she needn't get quite so close to Hunter right now, not when all she needed to do was discover if he were the warrior she sought. 'Twould be three weeks afore the next full moon rose, which meant three weeks until she'd know if a bond existed between them. A lifetime away, yet not so far. She would wait, as patiently as she could.

She breathed deep of the salty sea air, pushed away from Hunter and hunkered down into a crouch. With one palm pressed firm on the grass, she closed her eyes and allowed her senses to rise. Even though so far away from Gilleoin's time, she would still be able to sense her kindred fae kind she'd left behind, and she touched her heart as the steady thrum of her people rose and brought such sweet calm to her very soul.

Chapter 2

Hunter couldn't stop staring at Ailith as she crouched with her hand pressed to the shoreline. She'd had her hand curled around his bicep mere minutes ago, her fingers so small yet so warm and burning a brand into his skin. She was in heat too, unmated and now they'd left the great hall, her heady scent once again swirled on the breeze. So damn intoxicating. He drew it fully into his lungs and his bear rolled around deep inside him, his other half now incredibly content he had her all to himself where they could remain alone.

Those with the enchanted fae dust she held could spell all manner of things, from manipulating memories, cloaking their forms, to erasing their scent. Over the years, he'd read recorded accounts in their ancient tomes about the dust and the fae who wielded it. He hadn't heard about her specifically though, her father, aye. Cian was known as the greatest healer of their fae kind beyond the veil, the legends surrounding the prince immense.

He paced the shoreline right beside her, crunching the sand and pebbly stones under his feet. She was so trusting, what with giving him her back within minutes of meeting him, but it had felt incredibly natural to stand that way with her and when she'd leaned back and he'd wrapped an arm around her waist, heat had flared at the base of his spine, zapped around to the front and stiffened his cock. First time that had ever happened around another woman, and what a woman. She was beautiful. Her golden-brown locks fell in spiral curls halfway down her back, her nose dainty and the freckles across her high cheeks so cute. What he found the most striking though, was that she stood like a warrior, her battle leathers donned and a loose-sleeved cream tunic fluttering underneath the corseted leather bodice of her vest. The tips of her wrist daggers glinted under her cuffs, and the claymore belted at her side was a beauty. A finely made hilt of burnished steel with emeralds embedded in it, the stones an exact match to her emerald eyes, although her eyes also had flecks of gold within. Mesmerizing. He halted in front of her, lowered to a crouch and eye to eye, asked, "Do you sense anything? Is that the way of your skill? You connect with the soil and send your senses searching out?"

"Aye, and there are images unfurling, but still too gritty and dark to make out. I shall check again later." A stunning smile lifted her rose-pink lips, then she stood and ambled across to a washed-up log on the grassy verge. She eased down onto it, her booted feet wedged into the pebbly sand and the grass sprouting high behind her back. She patted the space beside her. "Come sit with me."

He wasn't turning that request down. He sat with his shoulder brushing her shoulder, scooped up a pebble and with his sight trained on the waves, head slightly angled, he sent the pebble skimming across the water. It tapped the surface, once, twice, three times, before disappearing into the white wash of a wave farther out from shore. He had so many questions for the woman beside him, and he needed to know more about her. He'd begin with the basics. "What's your favorite food?"

"Strawberries. Yours?"

"Pork and bacon. What's your favorite color?"

"Purple." She handed him another pebble. "Yours?"

"Emerald, the same color as your eyes." He sent the pebble skipping out across the waves, then when it got swallowed by the waters, he plucked another and sent it flying too. "Favorite time of the day?"

"Midnight. You?"

"There's nothing quite like sitting under a midnight sky with the moon shining and stars twinkling, so I would have to say the same. Favorite book?" he quizzed.

"Oh gosh, that's *Weaponry, Sight and Skill*. Have you ever read it?"

"I have. It's one of my favorites too. We've got an early edition of it in the clan library." It covered all the weapons across the centuries, the required skills needed to use them too. A woman after his own heart. "Have you ever kissed a man?"

"That would be telling." Brow arched, she wriggled around, slung one leg over the other side of the log and facing him, pressed her hands against the mossy bark. "I have a serious question now. Since you came of age, have you ever sensed even the slightest urge when the full moon rose to begin the chase for your chosen one?"

"No, unfortunately I haven't." He straddled the log too, his palms on the bark and his fingertips a mere inch from hers.

"What of Liam and Levi?" She looked deep into his eyes, focused nowhere but on him, and that much intensity punched him in the gut. In a good way, a fascinating way. His bear loved the way she watched him so intensely, as if trying to see deeper inside his very soul. He'd let her dive right in if she wished, and lock her in place so she couldn't escape.

"There have been no urges for them either, whereas I have a multitude all tumbling about inside me right now, and I have since I first caught the sound of your voice and your intoxicating scent from the battlements. I couldn't get inside fast enough to find out who had arrived." He breathed deep again, got another good lungful of her heavenly aroma and his bear fairly pushed against his skin to get closer to her. "Have you ever gotten this close to an unmated shifter?" he asked, all rumbly and rough.

She lifted her chin, licked her upper lip with a soft sweep of her enticing pink tongue. "There is Gilleoin and his sons, Kenneth and Ivan. I have spent a great deal of time with them, and I have known every chief of your clan since the beginning. Murdock has always been my favorite, although his and Cherub's need for secrecy until now has meant my visits here were kept in private and unspoken of. Glad I am, that is no longer the case. That I can sit here and freely speak to you."

"I wish I'd met you years ago, six years to be precise, when I first came of age."

"You're so young." She giggled, her merriment both lightening his heart and soaking deep within his soul.

"You don't look a day over twenty yourself."

"Aye, we cease aging from our twentieth year, but I can assure you, I am very, very, very—"

"Okay, I get the point. You're very old compared to me."

"Nay." She giggled again, wriggled closer until her fingertips touched his fingertips on the bark. She glanced between their hands and his face. "I was going to say very wise, and by the way, you should never call one of the ancient fae *old*. 'Tis rather disrespectful. My papa, if you'd told him that, would have sliced off your tongue."

"Would Cian have healed it afterward?" He wriggled his tongue inside his mouth, her words making it tingle with pins and needles.

"That would have depended on how remorseful you were afterward. Cian is a powerful healer, is the second-born child of Ailbert, the King of the Fae. My grandfather raised all his children with a stern hand, and in so doing, my papa did the same with me."

"Cherub isn't stern, and she's Ailbert's firstborn."

"She can be when she wishes to, particularly when the safety and protection of her people are at risk. She will attack without any hesitation if need be. Have you ever witnessed her might and strength in battle? She commands the very element of air, can whip it into a mighty storm unlike any you've ever seen. She can and does call forth wrath and destruction when pressed to. Unfortunately, though, my aunt and I must also take great care no' to kill those we meet while traveling through time. To do so can cause an adjustment, like ripples which can alter the very fabric of the future itself, which we try our hardest to steer well clear of doing, unless there is no other choice."

"But Cherub's such an adorable sprite, with her golden locks and glittery skin. She dresses like a lady at court, in fine gowns and such. One wouldn't think she could hurt a fly."

"You clearly have a lot to learn about Cherub. My aunt can be underestimated like that, but mark my words, she is a warrior through and through, the same as my sisters and I are." Leaning forward, she placed both her hands on his bare knees, her fingers curling into the hem of his Matheson plaid hooked around his waist and looped over one shoulder. "Do you believe in magic, Hunter?"

"It's hard not to considering the abilities and skills held by my clan, and the fact that we're shifters. I would say that you're rather magical to be around as well." He cupped her face in his hands, stroked his thumbs gently back and forth across her soft, creamy cheeks. "I also believe in love at first sight. That happened for my parents, and before the full moon rose too. They'd always gravitated toward each other as cubs, as teens as well, then once they reached adulthood, no one and nothing could halt them from completing the bond the first night the full moon declared they were soul bound."

"That is a rarity though. Never forget that." She pulled away from him, stood and ambled back down to the water's edge. She wandered along the shoreline, right where the waves washed in and left a line of foam before washing back out. She didn't stop, but kept walking and he bounded to his feet and jogged after her.

Coming in beside her, he asked, "Regarding your vision, have you seen when the Chief of MacKenzie intends on killing this warrior, the exact day and time?"

"Nay, but 'twill be soon. That is the way of my visions. Also, from their conversation, I'm aware the warrior perishes no' long after his torture begins. An hour to be precise, with the loss of his head. I hope future visions will alert me to more details. That is how they unfold."

"I'm sorry you saw such a…difficult vision." It had to have been heart-breaking to witness.

"My visions are all difficult to watch." She slowed her pace and stopped, then searched his gaze as if trying to see right into his heart, the moon lighting her golden hair like a halo over her head. "You must understand, Hunter, that I only ever see visions of war. That is the way of my combat skill. I shall also know if what I'm doing here in your time has a chance of altering the warrior's future simply through those visions."

"How exactly?" He lifted one of her golden spiral curls and wrapped the length around his finger.

"If I continue to see his death occurring, then I'll know I've changed naught, but if I see him alive and well instead, then I'll have fulfilled the purpose of what I've been called to do."

"Have you ever failed in fulfilling that purpose?"

"Never." She shook her head as if she never would either, not if she had her way. "This warrior I seek might be my mate. He said so in my vision of him, although only the full moon can truly verify such a bond. Still, I've been waiting over eight-hundred years for him, and if he is mine, then I willnae lose him afore our lives together have even begun."

If she was his mate, then he had no intention of losing her either. "War is damn destructive, no matter what era in time it occurs."

"Aye, war always lurks on the horizon though, for those on Earth." She watched him as he continued to play with the curl he'd wound around his finger.

"Sorry. I can't help but touch you. The urge is strong."

"'Tis all right." She waved his apology off. "I need to learn more about you in particular. I'm aware of course that your clan works high-level government cases which requires your specialized fae-shifter abilities, and that those cases can take you and your kin into places of war, both within your own country and across the seas. Are you a part of one of these teams?"

"Aye, war is ugly and brutal. Peace is what we're after, and we fight to ensure that peace for those who can't fight for it themselves."

"A noble cause, which is how I live my life as well, how my sisters and Cherub live it too." She caught his hand and turned it over before studying the lines across his palm. She traced across the deepest of the three most prominent lines before lifting her gaze back to his. "You hold a long life-line, but it has an intersection first afore it continues."

"What does that mean?"

"That your death is about to come, but it shall be circumvented. A good sign, one I pray remains true."

"Interesting."

"You, Hunter Matheson, might be the very warrior I'm seeking. In fact"—her gaze narrowed as she eyed him—"the longer we've talked, the more it makes sense. You must be the one I need to protect."

"Does that make me your future mate as well?"

"Only the full moon can confirm that possibility." She dipped two fingers inside her pouch and tossed her fae dust. It swirled all around him, then she uttered words he strained to catch, something about being very still, then something about forgetting all that had passed between them. Something more about forgetting her.

He blinked twice, hard, and turned in a slow circle.

His mind, incredibly fuzzy, throbbed as if he'd taken a hit to his head and gotten knocked out.

He plucked the sleeve of his white tunic and shimmery golden dust flickered in the moonlight then fluttered to the shoreline. Why was he down here?

2:00 AM glared back at him in red digits on his watch from under the backlit light.

His shift had finished an hour ago, yet he couldn't remember even one minute of the time that had passed since.

Growling low under his breath, he strode back toward the keep, bounded along the pine-needle strewn trail and caught an elusive fragrance drifting on the breeze. He halted and drew in a deep breath. Unmated female. Fertile unmated female. Shock slapped him hard in the face.

How was that possible? But more than that, why did the scent raise every hair on his arms and send his gut churning into a terrible mess?

He picked up his pace, loped through the postern gate then jogged across the inner bailey along the cobbled pathway. He skidded inside the front door of the keep, and caught a glimpse of a woman with golden spiral locks wearing battle leathers and a sword at her side. She disappeared up the stairwell.

Chase, his bear growled from deep inside him.

Gritting his teeth, he pounded up the stairs two at a time.

On the second floor, he halted, her elusive fragrance tickling his nose. She was close, incredibly close, and his bear rumbled and demanded he continue the hunt. The paneled hallway stretched out before him, although devoid of even one soul. He marched to the first chamber door and sniffed. Her scent didn't end here, but continued onward. Door after door, he checked for the fragrance he was after, then caught Cherub and Kirk's scent which surprised him. They must have arrived without him sighting their arrival. They certainly hadn't been here for the evening meal, just before he'd gone on duty. He passed his own chamber door, reached the last door along the passageway and snapped his teeth together as the woman's aroma ended directly at his feet.

He stepped back, until his back touched the wall across from the guest chamber, then he shucked his plaid, shirt, and boots before giving his body to his bear. Bones popped and a moment of pain flared through him as he made the Change.

His bear was riled, and he needed answers.

They both did.

Chapter 3

Gulping air, Ailith leaned against her door after she'd raced back from the beach and whipped inside. That had been one close call. She'd barely kept ahead of Hunter after she'd spelled him by the loch. She hadn't had a choice in removing his memory of their first meeting and conversation by the water, not when her duty was to ensure his survival. Aye, she was certain he was the warrior from her vision. His lifeline had indicated a great deal, and the way he'd spoken to her had tugged at her heart. So too, if she was being honest with herself, that tugging had begun back when she'd first met him in the great hall. The connection between them had built swiftly, progressing as they'd walked down to the waterfront, then surging ahead during their conversation. He'd captured her attention immediately, unlike any other man before him. That wasn't to say they were mated, but she hadn't been able to cease touching him, and he'd been much the same way with her. She'd loved it when he'd sat next to her on the log and given her his undivided attention, then played with a lock of her hair as they'd walked along the beach.

The moonlight had cast his handsome features into firm determination, highlighting the strong line of his jaw and casting a shimmery glow over his furrowed forehead and flaring nostrils.

Aye, they'd flared because he'd been breathing so deeply in order to take in more of her scent, and she hadn't missed that. She likely should have spelled the removal of her scent once her last spell within the great hall had worn off, only with him dragging in her scent like that, it had made her belly flutter with such excitement.

Aye, it still fluttered now. She squeezed her hands into fists and tried not to open the door and bound back out. She both wanted to be with him, and didn't. His safety was only assured if she set these rising emotions for him aside though, and returned to the past. She couldn't take him with her, and he wasn't permitted to follow. That was the only option moving forward, until she no longer saw a vision of him perishing.

The cracking of bones echoed under the door then the heavy thump and scratch of paws resounded. Shifters could be incredibly territorial and if they were mated, he would be even more territorial due to their bond. Somehow, he'd already tracked her down. Drat it all. She jiggled from foot to foot, so unsure as to what to do. Let Hunter come in and spell him to forget her again? Or ignore him?

More thumping and scratching, a bear's muzzle pressed to the gap under the doorway and a snort and growl rumbling through. Ugh, he wasn't leaving, not until she'd dealt with him again. Heart squeezing in on itself, she opened her door and leaned against the doorjamb, then tried her best to assert as much authority into her voice as she could. "What do you want?"

A big bear prowled back and forth, Hunter's clothing scattered across the floor of the passageway. He'd shifted in a hurry, and boy, did she have her work cut out for her with him. His bear's golden shifter eyes drilled into hers, his beast holding a stunning brown pelt with white-tipped paws.

He rumbled another grizzly growl, then padded past her into her chamber before turning around in a slow circle in the middle of the room at the end of her four-poster bed. He sat on his rump on the white rug, his front legs straight and ears alert as he observed her like one did when examining a bug under a microscope. Aye, and she was currently the bug.

"It appears we need to talk. Give me one moment." She didn't need to alert his clansmen to what was going on, which meant she needed to collect his clothing and remove any sign of his shift. She scooped his boots up, got one finger stuck under the large silver buckle on the front, a buckle engraved with the head of a bear. She pulled her finger free and sliced it almost to the bone. A hidden knife, a small one, was tucked underneath the silver. A warrior always carried a weapon on them which no one else could find. This must be his, the blade small but incredibly sharp. She sucked on her finger as she picked up his tartan and tunic, sword belt and weapons. Another finger wag at him. "Remain here."

Thankfully, he stayed put as she walked through the connecting bathroom and placed his weapons and clothes on the trunk at the end of his bed. She hurried back, her finger thankfully already healed, the skin having drawn together over the cut.

Across from her, Hunter maintained his state on full alert, his gums pulled back and sharp white teeth gritted together as he snarled, his golden gaze on her finger rather than her face. She held her finger toward him. "See, already healed. I'm an immortal. Never forget that, Hunter. I cannae be killed, whereas you can."

Carefully, she turned a touch and snuck more dust from her pouch, then tossed it over him. "Listen to me well. No more shall you recall why you're in my chamber, or the chase you've made. You shall instead feel sleepy, your eyelids weighing you down. Sleep now, Hunter, rest and recover from your night. You willnae awaken until after I have."

His bear blinked slowly, struggled to keep his eyelids open, then he slid down and slumped onto the mat.

She brushed her hands against her legs, a job well done. No one should ever mess with one of the ancient fae. Only now he lay sprawled across her chamber floor, cutting off her path to her bed. Oh well, she'd simply sleep in his bed instead. It mattered little where she did, only that come the light of the new day, she got out of here as quickly as she could. Home to her warrior encampment.

Sword unbelted and wrist daggers removed, she set her weapons on top of the vanity in the interconnecting bathroom, tugged off her boots and left them propped in one corner. She splashed water on her face from the tap and patted her cheeks dry with a cloth from the cupboard.

Inside Hunter's chamber, she crawled under the thick brown fur, plumped one white pillow and settled herself. Through the open doorway, Hunter still snoozed, his jaw slack and tongue lolling out. He appeared so content and she couldn't help but smile. Papa would tell her off for using her dust in such a manner, of removing her *possible* mate's memories of her. He preferred she and her sisters used their dust for only extreme emergencies, but Hunter had backed her into a corner and left her with no choice. Hopefully, he'd forgive her. Hunter and Papa both.

She pummeled the pillow and snuggled, the bedsheets carrying the tantalizing scent of the man she'd just spelled. The faint aroma of an ocean breeze swirled about her too. Mmm, wonderful.

Chapter 4

Hunter clawed the white woolen mat and perked his ears as the intoxicating aroma of an unmated female swarmed his senses. He fought the deep sleep, his mind all foggy and thoughts skewered. That scent meant huge things to him though, and his bear was tearing at him from the inside and demanding he awaken.

He pushed through the fog and heaved to his feet. All jelly-legged, paws scrabbling to stay upright, he wobbled into the bathroom and through the other door into his own chamber. His bear rolled his shoulders and tipped his head up. Difficult though. He wanted to slide back down onto his belly on the floor and snooze the rest of the night away. Good grief. It was as if someone had drugged him and he couldn't properly awaken.

Never had this happened to him before.

Ahh, there, he caught the mouth-watering aroma of unmated female and it revived him a bit. His bear dragged in a deep breath and slobbered all over the floor as he jerked wonkily toward the woman's slumbering form in his bed.

He bashed his tail end against the trunk as he passed it, then snapped his teeth at his butt. It was a pest for not obeying his directive to move. Never had he been so uncoordinated in his life. He bumped his head into the mattress, gave it a shake and returned his gaze to the woman under his bedcovers. He grinned sloppily. Goldilocks slept in his bed, but without the three bears—there was only one bear, him.

He heaved up and his paws thumped onto the mattress, most clumsily and nothing like his normal self, but thankfully his ungainly move didn't even cause her to flicker an eyelash. She was curled up on her side, her cheek resting in her open palm on his pillow and her breath whispered softly in and out from between her lips, and whoa, what incredibly alluring lips. So lush and pink and—his bear wanted to nibble, or just bite her, or perhaps nibble then bite, then eat her up as fast as he could.

Mmm, bet she'd make a tasty meal. He smacked his lips together. More drool plopped.

She had the cutest freckles dusting her cheeks and one golden ringlet had snagged on the end of her nose, the wispy strands fluttering across her lips as she breathed. Her long neck lay exposed, her pulse beating right there where he wanted to sink his teeth into her. Wait.

He jerked back. No, he wasn't permitted to sink his teeth into any woman, other than his mate. He snuck his muzzle into the deep V of her white tunic and licked across the curvy upper line of her breast. Unfortunately, her black leather bodice prevented him from going any farther down, but he'd gotten a good taste of her anyway. His bear loved the taste of her, all sweet and juicy, like a ripe melon waiting to be consumed on a sweltering summer day.

He lifted one paw and played with the dangling ties of her tunic, and she grumbled in her sleep and tried to swat his paw away. Hmm, she'd make a good playmate. He wanted a playmate, a woman who was all his, and he'd been waiting a hell of a long time to find one. She smelled just right too, purrrrfect, her clothes somehow already holding his scent, although perhaps from her falling asleep in his bed, because there was no other way for her to hold his scent otherwise. Unless of course he'd already tangled with her somehow. He shook his head of that thought. He'd never forget tangling with a woman like this. His yummy Goldilocks.

He pushed off the bed and lumbered across to his scotch chest. With a mere thought from his mind alone, he forced the Change in a bright flash of sparks, which thankfully didn't awaken Goldilocks. Without a noise, he opened the top drawer and pulled on his black silk boxers. He usually slept in the nude, but he'd need to make an allowance for her tonight. Carefully, he closed the navy curtains across his wide window and eased into bed beside her under the fur.

She let out a soft moan and rolled over, her hand settling on his chest and her cheek on his shoulder. Sweet heaven. He had to be dreaming. There was no other reason for this insanely beautiful moment other than that he'd dragged it straight from his fantasies. He closed his eyes, wrapped his arm around her waist and caressed the lower curve of her back. He tucked her in against him even closer, and his bear moaned so sweetly with satisfaction.

Aye, he loved holding her, touching her, being near her.

Mate, his bear rumbled.

Aye, she's our mate, he whispered back.

Chapter 5

The dawn's rising sunshine slithered through the slim gap in the heavy drapes over the window and Ailith blinked against the harsh light spearing right into her eyes. At her back, intense heat wrapped around her and she wriggled about and—how on earth had Hunter gotten into bed with her? Without her sensing it? She'd spelled him to fall asleep and he shouldn't have awoken before her.

Carefully, she pushed the fur cover back and oh my. He was nearly naked. All he wore were black silk boxers that barely covered his nether region, particularly since his shaft was erect and the head seemed intent on escaping the waistband. He had one sizeable cock for that to happen.

Eyes away. Look anywhere other than at him. Except she couldn't. Of course, she'd never lain with a man before, not since she'd been awaiting a mated bond to form between her and her chosen one, but she was certainly aware of what a man looked like, particularly when she'd spent so much time at the warrior encampment and the men there would undress and get stark naked before bounding into the loch for training. Some kept their breeches on, but most favored wearing naught at all, preferring no hindrance with clothing which might slow their speed in the water.

She wasn't unaware of how a man and woman joined together either, not when she'd lived as many centuries as she had. She'd come across her fair share of warriors coupling with wenches in darkened niches, either in the castle, stables, or deep in the woods. She'd even watched a few as they'd come together in a rowdy climax since she hadn't been unable to back away quick enough.

She reached with one finger and touched Hunter's chest. His torso tapered in a firm V downward, with twin ropes of muscle rippling down his sides. She smoothed her hand along his jaw, his morning stubble raspy under her fingertips. A wayward lock of his hair curled deliciously across his forehead, and she wrapped that curl around her finger then pushed her hands fully through his dark hair. So silky and soft. Tingles raced across her skin and made her nipples tighten.

His shoulders were so wide and thick with muscle. She glided around his flat male nipples. Both contracted into firm points and when she leaned in and flicked her tongue over one, he groaned in his sleep and tightened his hold around her middle.

Mmm, he tasted divine.

She wanted more.

She licked over his other nipple and heat flared through her core.

This could get rather addictive, rather quick. Not good. She had a mission to complete, and getting sidetracked wasn't permitted, not even by this tasty warrior.

She eased away from him, pried his fingers loose from around her waist and slipped out of bed. Without looking back, she hauled her butt into her own bedchamber.

"Ailith?" A knock rattled her door. "It's me, Isla."

"I'm coming." It had been months since she'd last seen Isla. Murdock's daughter was mated to Kirk's brother, Iain, and she and her chosen one had traveled to Gilleoin's time during Iain's chase of her. She opened the door and smiled at Isla standing with a duffel hanging over one shoulder and two steaming mugs in hand, a divine chocolate aroma swirling into the air from them.

"Dad said you might need some clothes, that you arrived last night without a bag." With her buttery-yellow blouse swaying over her pregnant belly, Isla extended one mug with a grin. "I come with hot chocolate too."

"Thank you, clothes would be wonderful, hot chocolate, divine." Even though she wanted to leave as soon as possible, she couldn't remain in these clothes which held Hunter's scent. Likely her hair and skin carried his alluring aroma too, so she would need to shower before stepping one foot out of this chamber. "I am terrible at procuring clothes with my dust. I always end up bringing forth the wrong things, like a broom instead of breeches, a tin can instead of a tunic." She accepted the mug, slid the duffel from Isla's shoulder and set the bag on top of the wooden trunk at the end of her bed, the quilted burgundy and white covers still pristine since she hadn't slept under them.

Isla closed the door and cast her gaze from her to her bed then back again. "I should probably warn you that Dad had another vision this morning."

"About the warrior killed by Colin MacKenzie?"

"No, about you and Hunter down at the loch. He saw you spelling the removal of Hunter's memories, of you bolting back here then getting chased down by Hunter." Barefoot, her red-painted toenails peeking out from underneath the bottoms of her jeans, Isla eased onto the bed, her drink sloshing to the rim as the base knocked against her belly. She giggled and drank a mouthful. "I'm not sure I'll be able to get back up again without a helping hand, so don't go too far."

"I'll remain close at hand." Grinning, she sat next to Isla and spread her hand over the rounded bump of her belly. One foot kicked her palm, then a second foot. Again, and again, she got pummeled by little feet. "You have two very feisty cubs in there."

"They get incredibly active whenever Cherub touches my belly just as you're doing right now. Dad said that's due to the ancient fae blood you and Cherub hold. It's stronger, richer, more magical. They can sense that."

"Aye, our ancient fae blood calls powerfully to those of our kind, even within the womb." She set her mug on the floor, leaned in and rested her cheek against the area where the babies' heads should be lower down on Isla's belly. A delightful thrum of angelic sweetness flared out and her heart lifted. Through her telepathic skill, she touched her mind to first one of the babe's and then the other's, then she touched Isla's mind and joined them all together. "*Little ones, I am Ailith. I cannae wait to meet you when you enter this world.*"

Gurgles resonated as Isla's sons wriggled about.

"Do you wish to speak to them?" She arched a brow at Isla.

"Good grief, I didn't know this would be possible." Tears swam in Isla's eyes.

"'Tis only possible because I'm a telepath with the ability to link those to me who dinnae hold that skill. They will be able to hear your voice once you speak mind to mind with them." To the babies, she murmured, "*Your Mama is eagerly awaiting your arrival.*"

More excited gurgles and swishing.

The tears in Isla's eyes flowed free. "*I love you both, just as your father loves you both.*" She hugged her belly, her love for her unborn children flowing along the merged connection and sweeping over her children. "I wish they could speak to me in return."

"That isnae possible, until they are much older." Ailith waited for the babies to settle back to sleep then she closed her connection with them and wiped Isla's tears from her cheeks.

"Have you heard why I'm here?"

"Aye, Dad left nothing out. All our clan are aware of the reason why you, Cherub and Kirk have arrived." She slanted her head. "Is that why you removed Hunter's memories and ran from him? Is he the warrior you saw imprisoned in your vision, who was slaughtered by Colin MacKenzie? Is he your mate?"

"He is the warrior from my vision, but I must wait until the next full moon to be sure if he is my mate as well. Neither of us can be certain until then."

"Hunter has never chased any woman the way he has chased you. Dad agrees with me too." Isla sipped her drink and rubbed her belly. "How do you really feel about him? Anything you say to me will go no further than these four walls."

"I find him incredibly distracting."

"Then you need to tell Hunter that."

"I'd be doing him a terrible disservice if I did, particularly when I intend on leaving."

"I find you incredibly distracting too." Hunter leaned against the bathroom doorway, arms lazily crossed, his feet and chest bare, and his kilt barely hanging onto his trim hips.

"You've been listening in?"

"From the moment you left my bed. You're Ailith, one of the ancient fae, who is terrible at procuring clothes with your dust. You love hot chocolate, and you've spelled the removal of my memories about you thus far. You're a telepath, who just connected Isla and her babies in a mind to mind conversation with you, and my chief had a vision that saw you running from me last night, and of me chasing you down. You wonder if we are mated, but won't know for sure until the next full moon, which explains why you slept in my bed. Oh, and apparently, I've featured in one of your visions, in which you saw me being slaughtered by Colin MacKenzie. Did I miss anything?"

"You won't be slaughtered by the MacKenzie, not when I intend on leaving and ensuring you can never travel to the past."

She stood and snorting, tried her hardest to give him her sternest expression. "When I said I find you incredibly distracting, I actually meant that in a bad way."

"You're in heat, Goldilocks." He gritted his teeth. "I could scent you a mile away, whether you were next door or not."

"Goldilocks? Why'd you call me that?"

"The name seems to suit you."

"Well, this Goldilocks holds the skill of combat sense and can receive visions of war afore they unfold. Unfortunately, I've foreseen your death, and now 'tis my duty to ensure your protection."

"I don't need anyone's protection."

"Aye, you do. I've foreseen—"

"I understood that part, you had a vision."

"I think that's my cue to leave." Isla grimaced as she rocked on her butt on the bed and tried to get up. She waved one hand at them. "Ugh, some help over here, please?"

"Allow me." Hunter whisked past her and offered Isla a hand up.

The perfect distraction, and exactly what Ailith needed. She scooped Isla's duffle and ducked into the bathroom, then flicked the lock on both doors and turned on the overhead light. She sagged against the vanity, her palms pressed to the marble countertop. The most difficult part of her journey here was now over. She could safety leave knowing she'd discovered who the prisoner was—Hunter Matheson. Now, she'd ensure his survival by whipping away just as swiftly as she'd arrived.

Certainly, for what remained of her time here, she'd simply keep her wits about her and remain as far away from Hunter as she possibly could. Showering and removing his scent from her was the first task on her immediate to-do list.

She stripped off her black leather breeches, vest, and cream tunic, tossed her clothing into the corner wicker basket and set her pouch on the counter so she wouldn't forget it. Each time she'd visited this century she'd always enjoyed the modern conveniences on offer, like hot running water. She opened the glass shower door and tipped the showerhead toward the tiled wall so she wouldn't get splashed with chilly water and lifted the lever. Water gushed out and as soon as the flow became warm, she tipped the showerhead back in place and stepped inside the cubicle and closed the door.

Steam swirled and she leaned into the water's heavenly warmth. From the shelf, she squirted liquid soap into her palm and frowned at the strange fragrance. *Bacon Scented Soap,* the label displayed. How unusual. Perhaps a manly scent. Oh well, she'd try it, particularly since she hardly wished to smell of fertile woman. From top to toe, she soaped herself clean then picked up the shampoo.

Good grief. *Pork Belly Shampoo.* Might as well lather up with that too. She'd be flavorsome meat running about on two legs, but what the heck. A dollop in hand, she scrubbed her hair then rinsed.

Done, she turned the lever off, wrung out her hair and opened the door. A plume of steam billowed and coated the large looking glass over the basin. She nabbed one of the plush white towels stacked on a wooden rack beside the vanity, wiped the glass and cleared the fog. She patted herself dry, hung the towel over the rail and flipped the top of the duffel. From inside, she pulled out a pair of modern jeans and a t-shirt. Perfect. She quite liked the jeans of this time, and she certainly preferred donning such clothes over gowns like Cherub did. Oooh, and underwear. She tore the plastic wrap from a packet holding a red pair. Cairstine adored this kind of frippery like she did, while Lilias not so much. Her youngest sister hardly wore much at all since she was always dipping and diving about in the water, the element she controlled through her fae skill.

She tugged the panties up, jiggled into the jeans and tucked the hem of the black t-shirt in, hooked her ever-present pouch through one belt loop, then strapped on her sword and wrist daggers, which she'd left on the countertop last night. A quick rummage through the top vanity drawer and she found a brush. Her hair always dried into bouncy spiral curls, which she usually left lying loose down her back, so she swept the brush through and left it at that.

From the drawer, she found a guest toothbrush and scrubbed her teeth clean, then she tidied the counter and left the duffel in the corner. Ear pressed to her chamber door, she caught no noise filtering through. Hunter surely would have used the hallway to return to his chamber by now.

She opened the door an inch. All was clear. Wonderful. She stepped across to the window and smiled while outside, a score of muscled men with bare chests and belted Matheson plaids partnered up and tapped their swords together. They swung, and the heavy clang of steel on steel ricocheted toward her. Dreary gray skies loomed overhead, not unusual for this time of the year. 'Twas overcast more than sunny during these cooler months.

"Ailith?" A hand closed over her shoulder.

She jumped and clutched her chest as she faced her nemesis. "Hunter, you shouldnae sneak up on a lass like that."

"I didn't mean to frighten you. Have you finished in the bathroom? I—" He frowned, sniffed, then frowned again. "Did you use the bacon soap on the shelf in the shower cubicle?"

"Aye." Butterflies abounded in her belly, his wide chest so close and his torso still bare, although he'd changed out of his kilt and now wore tan rawhide breeches, which still sat far too low on his hips. Eyes up. No ogling his body.

"There are all sorts of pretty pink soaps in the bottom drawer of the vanity for our female guests."

"I only opened the top drawer."

"You could also have used the *other* bottle of shampoo in the shower."

"What *other* bottle?"

"The one behind the meat scented one." He waved his nose over her head, an easy feat since he stood a good foot taller than her. "Aye, that's pork belly I can smell. They're both gifts from Bella. My favorite food is pork and bacon, thus the reason for those scented products."

"Oh, of course it is." She clicked her fingers. "You told me so last eve. That those were your favorite foods."

"Speaking of last eve." He released a low growl, and she side-stepped.

"Don't move." He followed her and leaning in, dipped his head and trapped her easily between him and the wall. "You can't go downstairs smelling this good. You'll cause a stampede, one with claws coming out."

"I'd hoped to mask my scent by using the soap and shampoo, not make myself more alluring."

"I can help change your alluring state if you wish."

"How?"

"It'll be best if I show you, rather than tell you." He pressed closer until they were cheek to cheek, then he rubbed his body fully against hers.

"What are you doing?" She tingled everywhere they touched, warmth shooting to her core and making her nipples ping to attention.

"Embedding my scent into you. My kinsmen will now think twice before attempting to touch you."

Oh goodness. He was too close. She grasped his shoulders and bit into her bottom lip. "Please, you must stop."

"Not yet." A soft purr rumbled deep in his chest. "You still need more of my scent on you."

Her mind fuzzed and she swayed.

"My bear likes you."

"That'll be the pork and bacon speaking to him."

"He wants to take a bite out of you." He nipped her ear. "I

have a request."

"I'm no' entertaining any requests at present."

"I want my memories back. Can you restore them the same way that you took them from me, with your faerie dust?"

"Aye, but 'tis best I dinnae." He already knew the basics anyway from overhearing her conversation with Isla, and she didn't want him learning anything more.

"I can't stand not knowing what's already happened between us."

"I can offer compensation."

"In what form?"

"A new memory I won't take from you." She reached up on her toes and kissed his cheek, then settled back down and dragged in a hopeful breath. "There, will that do?"

"It's a start." A very satisfied grin lifted his lips.

"I'm sure I smell exactly like you now." This man was too much of a temptation. "You should finish dressing. Donning a shirt would be helpful. Cover up well, a jacket too." She motioned out the window where a hazy mist had now swept in, the clouds overhead darkening further. "A storm is brewing."

"As they always do in these parts." He stepped back, thankfully, although his smoldering golden gaze remained on hers.

"That-away." She pointed at their connecting bathroom. "Go."

"I'll go, but come and talk to me while I pull on a shirt." He turned and strode into his chamber as if she would follow his every command.

She released a long, unsteady breath then drat it all, she did indeed follow him. Like a lamb to the slaughter, she walked through the bathroom then stopped in the doorway while he foraged through his dresser. He flapped out a navy tunic with billowy sleeves, lifted his arms and let the soft cotton swish over his head. He tucked the hem into his breeches, the loose tunic ties swaying, the deep V of the neckline showing off far too much of his gloriously muscled chest.

"Allow me." She dragged the ties together and knotted it tight under his neck. "There we go. That's much better."

"I still need to breathe." He coughed, one finger tugging the neckline looser, amusement flickering in his eyes.

"Breathing is overrated." Best she brought whatever it was between them back to friendship, and fast. She slapped his arm as her fellow warriors often did with each other. "Are you joining your kin for training? You'll need your sword if you are."

"I'll join them after I've eaten breakfast with you." From on top of his trunk, he picked up his weapons, strapped on a wrist dagger and his sword belt.

"No need to join me for breakfast. I already have a date with Levi."

"You better not."

"He calls me his sweet pea."

He stared at her lips, her eyes, then her lips again, and for the life of her she couldn't move an inch. Good heavens, she needed to get out of his room, immediately. More heat pooled between her thighs and he breathed deep, his eyes slowly closing. He brushed up against her, and she fisted his shirtfront as he tipped her backward and pressed his cheek against her cheek, his lips a mere inch from her lips.

She couldn't move, not if the castle was on fire and burning down. Three more blasted weeks and she would know if he was truly hers, meanwhile she was one-hundred percent certain he was the warrior she sought, which meant leaving so she could ensure his protection. "I, ah, I want things right now that I shouldnae be wanting with you, Hunter."

"Trust me, I believe we both want the same thing." A long growl rattled from his chest and escaped his lips, beautifully full lips she wanted on hers.

"I want a mate who is all mine, who I can claim in every way." The truth, right from her heart, which she shouldn't be sharing with him, not right now, only she couldn't help herself.

"Then we definitely want the same thing, of which I'm certain you're looking at the man you're mated to." He curled his palm around her nape, his fingers warm and firm on her skin as he drew her even closer, then he angled his head and covered her mouth with his.

His kiss swept her away, sending a wave of dizzying sparks through her body, and goodness, his mouth was so achingly soft against hers. He parted her lips with his tongue and swept inside. He tasted her with gentle strokes and she clung to him, desperate for even more.

"Hunter?" His very stiff erection jabbed into her belly and she sighed with utter delight. Completely and utterly helpless to resist his touch, she rocked her hips against his hips. So sublime, and exactly what she needed. Such a depth of need overtook her.

"We wouldn't be touching like this unless we're mated." Hunter carried her one-step back to the wall, pressed her back against it then made love to her mouth with great care and devotion. Such a master of seduction, and she was falling fast. "You're mine, Ailith." He gripped her bottom and lifted her higher against the wall, his bicep muscles bulging as he raised her to his height. He kissed her deeply, every inch of his body surrounding hers.

Trapped. She couldn't move, not that she wanted to, so she hooked her legs around his hips and ground her lower body more deeply against the fierce heat he emitted.

Another rough and incredibly skilled kiss as he pushed his tongue into her mouth, and oh sweet heaven, she wanted to kiss him just as roughly in return. She yearned for more of this.

She yanked his tunic's hem from his breeches, smoothed over his lower abs and as she did, he kissed her as if breathing life into her. "We should stop," she murmured against his lips.

"Aye, we should, but I can't." He moved his mouth from hers, down her neck until he drifted over her pounding pulse point. He licked her skin, his tongue raspy and warm and then he scraped his teeth back and forth over her sensitive flesh. "I need to bite you, Goldilocks."

"I'm too hot."

"I like that you're hot, and I still need to bite you." He unzipped and opened her jeans, slid his hand down and rubbed her tight nub through her silk panties, then with his teeth on her neck, he bit down and she shuddered as her core rippled over and over with a fierce orgasm that took her breath away.

In a daze, she held on tight as he carried her to his bed. He dropped her lightly on the mattress on her back then stood over her. He thrust one hand down his pants and gripped his shaft, his body humming with power and his gaze locked on hers. "I wish to mate with you."

"We dinnae know if we belong together, and we willnae until the next full moon." She shoved up onto her elbows. "We should wait."

"Or not wait." He pressed his knees into the mattress either side of her hips, his hands either side of her head as he knelt over her. "When our shifter kind join as one with our true mate, we forge a merged link of the mind. It's inherent in our shifter blood, which means we'll know if we're mated far sooner than the next full moon if we join fully together right now."

"Have you forgotten, Hunter? I'm a telepath and can forge that merged link of the mind with you right now if I wished. You saw me do so with Isla and her babies."

"Damn."

"Let me show you." She activated her telepathy, touched her mind to his and whispered along the private pathway, *"You're one insistent bear, but 'twill be three weeks until you sense the need to hunt me. I will return by that time, to make sure I'm here and close. That isnae so long to wait considering you've already waited six years and I've waited over eight-hundred."*

"I love hearing you in my mind." Smiling, he leaned in, touched the tip of his nose to the tip of her nose. *"I'm not a telepath, but I will be able to connect to my mate's mind once we join together. That ability is inherent in my shifter blood, to forge and hold that connection with our chosen one. I say we join together now and see if I too can connect with you. That will prove one way or the other if we're mated."*

"If you're wrong and we arenae mated, then we can never reverse what we've done." They had to wait. There was no other way. She broke their link, shut their connection down. "I'm sorry. This is all my fault. I never meant for any of this to happen. I should have spelled the removal of your memories again after you overhead Isla and me talking."

She pushed against his shoulders and thankfully he rolled onto his back and away to the other side of the bed. Hands linked behind his head, he breathed deep, jaw clenched as if he tried to restore some control.

"You'll need to shower again," he muttered. "Otherwise I'm going to be all over you in two seconds flat."

"Consider it done." She bounded into the bathroom, closed the door and stripped off. A quick raid of the bottom vanity drawer secured her a pink bar of soap and she jumped in the shower and scrubbed her skin until it was almost raw. The *other* bottle of shampoo, which happened to be strawberry scented, got scrubbed through her hair and once she was all clean and smelling girly again, she emerged from the steamy confines of the shower and dried herself. Her clothing would still hold his scent as well, so she rummaged through the duffel and tipped out the only remaining clothing from within.

Gah, a gown. 'Twas beautiful though, that she couldn't deny. No underwear left, so she dragged on the forest-green fabric trimmed with brown fur around the hem and neckline and thrust her arms through the sleeves which draped over the backs of her hands. The velvet skirts brushed her ankles and she eased the matching slippers on since her boots just wouldn't suit. She'd do pretty for this morning.

A knock rattled the door. "We need to talk about what just happened."

"Nothing happened."

"Everything just happened." He opened the door and stepped inside. Agony tore at his face and made her heart squeeze.

"I'm sorry. This is all my fault." Clutching her bodice to her chest, she gave him her back. "Please, laces. I cannae reach them."

"Will you still be in heat in three weeks?" He tightened the laces then once done, turned her around by her shoulders, dipped his head and pressed a soft kiss against her neck.

"Hunter." She'd wanted to snap his name out, instead it had come out all sultry.

"I didn't mean to do that." He held his hands up as he took a step back. "I couldn't help myself. Tell me about your cycle."

"They fall twenty or so years apart, and I'm only ever in heat for a week at most. 'Tis one of the frustrations of my fae kind, that even with the extended length of our cycles, all the time we have to conceive is a similar length of time to that of a normal human woman."

"I don't want to wait another twenty or so years to conceive a child with you. Unless…" A deep smile lifted his lips, a naughty smile.

"Cease smiling at me like that. It isnae very helpful." She strapped her wrist daggers and sword in place, stuck her pouch in her pocket then ducked into her chamber and hurried down the passageway.

"I'm smiling because I've finally found my mate and nothing could make me happier." He kept an easy pace one step behind her.

"Stop following me."

"You are so stubborn."

"I could say the same about you."

He chuckled and jogged around in front, then cut her off before she could reach the stairwell. Blocking her path, he crossed his arms, spread his feet wide on the blue and green runner and gave her a very hungry-bear smile. "I need to know everything there is to know about you."

"I get very angry when constantly contradicted, or if my requests are ignored."

"You can guarantee I'll never ignore you." He tapped her nose. "Your current requests though, I completely disagree with. You want to run, and I want to put my hands on you, my lips too. My cock is also still rather hard and I want to put that deep inside—"

"Hunter Matheson!" She slipped a pinch of faerie dust from her pouch, slapped a hand against his chest and sent her gold dust fluttering over him. "Listen to me well. You will remain right here while I leave. You will also ignore any urge to follow me, and your cock will deflate and go all soft and you will totally forget about wanting to put it anywhere near me. Have I made myself clear?"

"Don't do this to us, Ailith. You are my responsibility, mine to protect and care for."

"Nay, you are mine and now I've found you, I will ensure your protection."

Chapter 6

Ailith hurried through the foyer toward the large oak doors leading into the great hall. Behind her, Hunter's fierce growl rumbled from the top of the stairwell and she checked over her shoulder as he pounded down the stairs. Good grief. He shouldn't have had any urge to follow her. "Leave me be, Hunter."

"You're asking the impossible."

Breathing deep, she pushed against the carved wooden doors engraved with the clan chief's arms, that insignia carrying two bears as supporters either side of it. The Gaelic words for Matheson, Son of the Bear, "Mic Mhathghamhuim," were emblazoned underneath. Gilleoin's shifter line had blended with her fae line and 'twas this clan she'd given her oath to guard and protect. Clan Matheson must survive and thrive, and never fall asunder. She'd win this current battle with Hunter too, and before this day was done.

She stepped inside the great hall abuzz with chatter. A good hundred of Hunter's kinsmen sat eating at trestle tables, then as they caught her arrival—and likely her huffing breath—those faces all turned toward her. "Ah, good morn, everyone." She waved a hand. "I'm Ailith."

"She's also my mate." Hunter wrapped an arm around her waist from behind, his warm breath fanning the top of her head and tickling strands of her hair across her cheeks. "I'm also certain of that, but I will have my work cut out for me convincing her. That being the case, I would appreciate as much aid as possible from you all."

"Wait." She held up both hands. "Hunter simply hopes I'm his mate, but as you are all aware, shifters must wait until the full moon afore you can truly know if you've found your chosen one, so for now his decree is mere speculation alone. He does no' require your aid at all." She slipped out of Hunter's hold and made a beeline for the trestle table overflowing with breakfast foods. Before the first table where the plates were stacked, she scooped one up and caught the glimmer from the precious gems sparkling within their Matheson clan shield hanging in pride of place on the wall where all could see it. Diamonds, rubies and yellow and blue sapphires sparkled along the silver edge and she touched one finger to the diamond sparkling the brightest in the center. This shield hung in Gilleoin's time in the same spot as well and she'd often admired its beauty. Hunter eased in beside her and she couldn't help but share her first memory of seeing it with him. "Did you know this shield was handcrafted by one of Gilleoin's favored blacksmiths, and the gems were gifted to him by David of Scotland in the late eleven-hundreds?"

"No, and do you mean David of Scotland, as in the Scottish prince and the eighth Earl of Huntingdon?"

"Aye, that is the David I speak of."

"Did you know him? You almost speak as if that's the case."

"Of course, I did. Afore his death, he was a most youthful man, a strong warrior and defender of those who couldnae fight for themselves." She'd never forget the great siege of the year 1194 which had involved David. She'd had a vision that one of his warriors, who held a touch of fae blood, was about to perish in battle and well before his time.

"Tell me. Is it true then?" Hunter leaned in, his words whisper-quiet.

"Is what true?" she whispered in return, not sure why they were whispering when shifters who held such good hearing were sitting so close by.

"Legend says David was Robin Hood." He cocked one eyebrow as if waiting for her confirmation of the truth.

"Oh, well, David certainly took part in the great siege of Nottingham Castle where the High Sheriff of Nottinghamshire and Derby County was taken captive. I was called, through my skill, to ensure the survival of one of his warriors at that time. I have been to places and times you could only dream of."

"That's for sure."

"Legend too says David's son, Robert, who unfortunately died young, might also have been Robin Hood." She cupped his cheek in one palm and smiled, the mischievous nature she occasionally held in check flowing forth. "Would you like to know which man was the true legend, and if I told you, would you keep it to yourself?"

Every ear of his clan was turned their way.

"Of course. Was it the elder, or the younger?"

She frowned and tapped her head. "Hmm, I suddenly have a memory block."

"You do not."

Giggling, she handed him her plate and collected another before wandering along the table holding an array of breakfast foods.

"You are incredibly annoying." He stroked one hand down her back then settled his palm on her hip.

"I know. Get used to it."

"I intend to." Said with a snarl and a caress over her hip. "What tempts you here?"

"Everything." Steam curled from a deep metal dish holding

bacon and sausages, which released a heavenly aroma that made her belly rumble. Potato hash overflowed the next dish, and a lass in short skirts topped the last platter of scrambled eggs with more from a pan she held. "This looks delicious, and I have no' eaten since lunchtime yesterday. We fae can get quite sidetracked and miss meals all over the place."

"I'd love to enjoy a meal alone with you, just the two of us, perhaps a picnic lunch somewhere along the shoreline in a secluded spot, or if you prefer a meal at one of the quaint restaurants in the village. We could call it our first date."

"Spending time alone with you could be dangerous. I also dinnae intend to be here for long enough to allow for a date."

"I intend for you to be around for dozens of them." He chuckled, his lips gliding across her neck as he crowded her from behind. "There's warm toast and an assortment of cereals and fruits on the next table."

"So I've noticed. Hold out your plate and I'll serve us both." She loaded their plates with the hot offerings and he plucked a hash brown from one dish and munched on it.

"I wish you'd serve yourself up on a plate for me," he murmured around his mouthful.

"Would you stop making such comments." She checked, and aye, they were still the center of attention. "Naught is going on here." She waved to everyone. "Continue with breaking your fast."

He chuckled some more.

She snorted under her breath and marched to the next table, poured puffed wheat into a bowl and sprinkled diced apricots on top. Breakfast in hand, she weaved around the trestle tables and when she spied Levi, she hurried across to him and set her cereal and hot plate on the table. She popped a kiss on his cheek, primarily to annoy Hunter, which it did going by the feral growl emanating from him back at the servery.

He hauled it across to her with lightning-fast shifter speed.

"Hands off her, Levi."

"I haven't got my hands on her." Levi thrust them in the air for proof.

"How are you this morn, Levi?" She smiled sweetly at the warrior.

"Almost about to get killed if you don't give me some slack. If Hunter says you're his mate, then you're his mate. The rest of us have to accept that."

"Well, whether we are mated or no' is still undecided." She added a splash of milk to her cereal from the jug in the center of the table, while Levi bit into his toast smeared in jam. "I have a request." She smiled sweetly at him again.

"I can accept requests, provided they're in line with clan rules."

"I need you to keep Hunter busy after I've left."

Another fierce growl and Hunter thumped his plate down on the table across from them. He stared Levi in the eye, the kind of stare that could slay a man without even the need for touch.

"Except that one." Levi pushed his chair farther from hers, the screech of wood across wood pitched high, Levi's answer too.

"There's no need for me to dally here now I know who I need to protect, that being Hunter, in case I didnae make that clear. I must return to the warrior encampment where I came from. My sisters await me in Gilleoin's time."

"Are they mated? Sassy like you?" A flirty spark lit Levi's eyes. "Fierce and protective too?"

"They arenae mated, and aye, they are sassy, fierce, and protective, just like me."

"Can I come with you? I want to meet them."

"Nay, I need you here to look after Hunter."

"You're not leaving through a portal without me." Hunter fisted a bacon strip and tore into it. He gnawed away like an angry bear who'd gone a week without food.

"I am." She poured cider into her mug and gulped. "Colin MacKenzie is waiting to strike. I can sense it to the depths of my bones. He has always desired this land and the strategic position held by this clan where the waterway between us and the Isle of Skye joins. Taking control of the main sailing route this keep overlooks is a prize to behold and that's what he is after. He willnae give up that desire."

"The MacKenzie has always been a thorn in our clan's side." Levi stirred sugar into his coffee, took a gulp and made a face while blowing out hot, steamy air. "Hot, hot. I don't know why I always have to scald my tongue."

"Good morning, all." Cherub breezed in and squeezed her shoulder, the long draping sleeves of her regal burgundy gown accented with gold satin fluttering over her wrists. "Did you sleep well, my dear?"

"Nay, Hunter is a beast to lie beside."

"You'll need to get used to that." Hunter stabbed a wedge of his sausage, smeared it through the ketchup on the side of his plate and chewed with a look that said, *Try and change that and we'll be having words.*

"Here are the facts," she stated to Cherub, ignoring Hunter entirely. "Hunter is the warrior from my vision. He's also certain we're mated, no' that he can know such information this soon. The full moon is some weeks away as you're aware, and until that time when he senses the urge to begin the hunt, then his declaration is mere speculation alone."

"Interesting, and aye, 'tis too soon for him to know if a bond has been forged, although"—Cherub thumbed her chin, her golden locks pinned back in a braid and her sparkly skin shimmering as she switched her gaze to Hunter—"Kirk's brother, Finlay, did in fact first sense his bond taking form with Arabel afore the full moon arose. Of course, he'd been searching for her for years, always being led to a place where he couldnae find her, and all because she didnae reside in this twenty-first century time but instead far in the past. Hunter, you've no' once sensed that kind of urge, which means either Ailith was beyond the veil every time the full moon rose these past six years, or you're no' actually mated."

"We're mated." He gave Cherub a firm look. "A man knows when he is." Then he leaned lazily back in his chair, stretched his legs out under the table and hooked one foot around Ailith's foot. "Goldilocks, I've been enamored by you from the moment we first met. Try to deny it."

"I—I—you are so annoying." She pushed her chair back and disengaged her leg. "Cherub," she bit out as she hooked one arm through her aunt's. "We need to speak. In private."

"As you wish." Cherub walked with her out the front door and they got enveloped in a mist which had thickened significantly since she'd last seen it rolling in out her chamber window. Now, she could barely make out the warriors training across the far side of the courtyard.

Eyeing her aunt, she asked, "Where's Kirk? We need to get out of here, as quick as we possibly can."

"Kirk and I stopped by Murdock's solar to speak to him afore breakfast and Kirk remained there for a chat, while I came downstairs to seek you out. Murdock mentioned his vision, that he saw you removing Hunter's memories by the loch then Hunter chasing you back inside."

"That certainly happened, and I had no choice but to remove Hunter's memories. He believes we're mated and he's insistent about returning with us to the past." She crossed the bailey and passed underneath the arched entrance, just as a guardsman waved to Cherub from his spot next to the two-story gatehouse. Cherub waved back, and she did too. "Is it possible for us to leave as soon as Kirk is free?" she asked her aunt.

"Nay, and I'll explain why. Murdock also reported to me and Kirk of a secondary vision he had this morning. He insisted we remain here for a little longer, even insisted 'twas imperative, that we must wait until you and Hunter have fought a battle, one which you must both undertake in order to reach a joint resolution."

"What kind of battle?" She shivered against the chilly wind.

"One that leads you to Faodail."

"A lucky find." Frowning, she translated the Gaelic word with ease, then continued, "We've already battled."

"Aye, but only with words. Murdock has seen you two battling with swords."

"Well, I'd love to take my blade to Hunter's backside. I'd strip a bit off here and there."

Cherub laughed. "That I cannae wait to see."

"I could show you right now, then we could be gone." She weaved past the stables and horses grazing at the feed trough, then veered along the grassy trail leading down to the loch. Waves crashed into shore and the tall pines swayed and creaked. A hawk squawked somewhere high overhead and with another gust, her hair whipped across her face.

"Since we're here, on the shore"—Cherub motioned to the sand and pebbles underfoot—"you should seek out with your senses and see if another vision is close."

"Aye, you're right. There might be an update." She longed to have a vision which no longer showed Hunter's death. If that happened, then she'd most certainly set his path back on the right course. She crouched and the ground moved and surged under her feet, a clear sign a vision awaited her. She planted her palms down and images rushed forth. Blood-red splattered across her sight.

"Ailith, what do you see?" Cherub wrapped one arm around her shoulders as she hunkered down next to her.

"Naught yet, but 'tis coming." Through the bloody haze, the Chief of MacKenzie emerged and she clutched ahold of the image and followed him as he stormed down the center aisle of a war galley in black boots, his claymore holstered to his back and his beady gaze pinpointed on her. A jagged scar sliced through his left eyebrow, his long war braids whipping about each side of his shaggy brown head. He leaned over her where she lay on the hard planks in the hull, then kicked her leather-clad legs apart and planted one foot between them.

Water sloshed about her and she searched amongst the thirty or so warriors seated on the benches all around. The men slashed their oars through the rolling waves, the wind filling the sail and a mist lingering in the air. Why the hell was she on board MacKenzie's vessel? She eyed him, face to face. "Where are you taking me, MacKenzie?"

"To my stronghold." MacKenzie snapped his teeth together and snarled. "I willnae be defeated, and certainly no' by the fae who've aligned themselves with Gilleoin. You Mathesons are well aware I want control of the waterways along this loch and for that I need Gilleoin's lands on the tip. I will hold dominion over these Western Isles and you're going to aid me in gaining the power and authority I seek." He spat on the boards beside her feet. "The warriors at the encampment were guarding you well during the battle. Particularly that one." He jabbed a finger over her shoulder, although she didn't turn.

Never had she given her enemy her back, and she didn't intend on beginning now. She needed to spell herself free of this place and be done with him. She grabbed her pouch, but MacKenzie snatched it from her hand and tossed it overboard. She had no weapons either, her sword and daggers gone.

"You're now mine," he bit out from between gritted teeth.

"I belong to no one." She shoved to her feet, wobbled on a loose plank and fell back into a large bundled lump. Two booted feet stuck out one end of the rolled plaid and, oh goodness. Those boots. They had silver buckles with the engraved head of a bear etched into them. Hunter's boots.

She heaved the rolled bundle over, the tartan unwrapping and the damp folds of wool falling away. Blood and dirt covered

Hunter's chest, an arrow sticking out, the tail end snapped off and the head protruding out his side. It had surely taken his life. She grasped his chilled face in her hands and screamed his name.

"Ailith!" Cherub squeezed her shoulders. "What have you seen? Tell me."

"'Tis Hunter." She shoved the blood-red of her vision away. "I've still seen his death. He's on board Colin MacKenzie's war galley, which means nothing I've done so far has altered his future. He still ends up in the past with me, although this time he perishes in another way. An arrow to the chest."

"Of course, I'll always end up in the past with you." Hunter bounded in, his dark hair blowing in the wind and his shifter eyes blazing a fierce golden hue.

Chapter 7

"Your visions prove we are soul bound." Intense and fierce emotions barreled through Hunter as he aided Ailith to her feet. "Nothing you can say or do will halt me from remaining at your side, whether here in this time or far in the past."

"Nay, my visions prove that war and destruction is about to unfold, that death is coming for you, one of my own fae-blooded kind. My responsibility is to ensure your protection, which means leaving you behind here in your own time. There's no other alternative."

"You've tried to leave me behind by removing my memories, yet my bond with you continues to grow and it won't be denied." When he'd awoken that morning at movement beside him, a woman with golden spiral curls had snuck out of his bed, her heavenly scent surrounding him and his memories missing from the night before. He'd hauled on some pants and tiptoed after her, then waited in the shadows of the bathroom while she'd opened her chamber door to Isla. He'd heard their conversation, had pieced together all that had happened, then when he'd come face to face with her, she'd invoked emotions within him he couldn't deny. Touching her, holding her, kissing her. It had been all he'd desired to do. Now though, he needed to protect her, to keep her close, to ensure their bond had time to gain in strength so he could convince her of exactly why they needed to remain together.

Instead, she appeared ready to run again. With her forest-green skirts in hand, she trekked up the grassy embankment then over her shoulder, muttered, "What are you doing out here? Spying on me?"

"I live here, and the weather is turning." He snorted and stomped after her. "From this moment forth, we shall remain at each other's sides."

"We willnae."

"You need to cease arguing with me." He strode past her, turned around and blocked her path.

"Out of my way." She glared at him, one hand fumbling to find the hilt of her sword within her long skirts. "Gah, this is why I rarely wear gowns."

"You are one very frustrating woman."

"And you are one very vexing man." She slid her wrist dagger free instead and pointed the razor-sharp tip in front of his nose. "Step clear, right now."

"Excuse me, you two." Cherub cleared her throat and tapped her head. "Kirk calls out to me along our merged link and I must go to him. I'll leave you both to sort out your differences. Dinnae forget though, Ailith, there shall be a battle of swords. We cannae leave until after that." Cherub dissolved into a mist and streamed away, her essence becoming as one with the haze shrouding them.

There was no other choice left to him. He needed to get Ailith away somewhere quiet, where the two of them could continue bonding. He'd promised her a trip to the village to see the restoration work underway and there in that place, they could be alone. No teams worked on the site today. First though, he needed to learn about this latest vision she'd had since it had riled her up all over again.

"This is so frustrating." She slid her dagger away.

"It doesn't have to be, not if we take the time to listen to each other." He grasped her hands and thumped them against his chest, then covered them with his hands to keep them pinned in place. "Nothing feels right unless I'm with you, Ailith. Tell me about your vision so we can come up with a plan. What have you now seen?"

"You still die, but this time in a different way, and 'tis all my fault." She scrunched her fingers into his navy tunic, bumped her forehead against his chest and released a low growl that spoke to the very heart of his inner bear. "I've always longed for a mate and if you are mine, then I have no intention of losing you at our enemy's hand."

"You feel it too, the mated bond tugging us closer together?"

"Nay."

"Be honest with me."

"What I feel is frustration, deep and intense frustration."

"So do I." Sliding his arms around her, he kissed the top of her head and tried to ease her distress. With her this close, his own frustration slowly dissipated, and in its place wonderful, serene satisfaction hummed through him. Losing her to another time wasn't an option, not now he'd finally found her. "We need to work together to alter this difficult future you see for me."

"'Tis no' difficult, but deadly. Colin MacKenzie wishes for control of the waterways between him and his enemy, and for that he needs Gilleoin's Matheson lands on the tip of Loch Alsh. He intends on holding dominion over the Western Isles," she mumbled into his shirtfront then lifted her gaze to his, "and he believes I'm going to aid him in gaining that power and authority he seeks. I have seen your death, first in the MacKenzie's dungeons, and now on board his war galley." She stuck her adorable chin out and glared down her nose at him even though he stood taller than her by a good foot. She was his little spitfire, and damn it, that obstinate look in her eyes stirred him deep within, in a way he could never explain.

"Where you go, I go." He would have his work cut out in convincing her of their bond and of his need to remain at her side, but he would. He simply needed time alone with her, and he intended on claiming that time now. He lifted her up, tossed her over his shoulder then with one hand across the back of her knees and the other clasped over her pert bottom, he strode into the misty depths of the forest and followed the inland trail leading toward the point of the bay, where the ruins of the village now sat with one home restored.

"Hunter, where are you taking me?"

"Where I promised to take you yesterday, the village."

"I'm sure there's a better way to carry me than this. Put me down, you big oaf." She thumped his backside with her fisted hands and his bear rolled around inside him with delight.

Aye, no matter how she touched him, he and his bear both adored it. He rubbed her backside and an intoxicating, warm honey aroma swirling with strawberries swamped his senses. Heavenly. Fur rippled down his arms and across his back, there one moment then gone the next.

"Oh my, is that your bear?" She tugged the hem of his tunic up and ran her hand over his bare back. "I'm certain I just felt fur here."

"Aye, it's my bear, but he can't have his freedom right now, not when I have yet to convince you that you're ours." His claws sliced out and his jaw popped. More fur rippled.

"I understand if you need to shift. My sister Cairstine holds the fae skill of morphing and makes the Change often into her favored form of the golden eagle. The urge strikes her hard and fast at times."

"As long as I'm touching you, my bear will eventually settle." He picked up his pace through the cloying fog and jogged through the underbrush, the swaying boughs of the pines brushing his arms on both sides of the trail, while high overhead the skies darkened into a churning, stormy black.

"'Tis about to rain, Hunter."

"Aye, I'll take a shortcut underground so we can remain dry. There's a tunnel leading to the village not far from here." Thunder rumbled, the trees whizzing by as he secured his hold on her, the entrance to the tunnel that ran underground to the village just around the next bend.

"I'm getting dizzy, extremely dizzy." She gripped his shoulders, pushed herself upright and slid down his front. He caught her in his arms and she looped her hands around his neck, her golden curls whipping all about in the whistling wind. Pine needles whisked across the forest floor and leaves crunched under his booted feet. Thunder boomed and lightning sizzled across the churning skies.

"Keep your head down," he ordered.

"I wish to see where we're going."

"Must you argue with me on every single issue?"

"Aye, I can be a touch argumentative at times, but 'tis an excellent quality to hold and shows I can speak my own mind. You should be grateful."

"I had no idea someone could actually argue their case about being argumentative." He chuckled as he tucked his chin over the top of her head and pumped his legs faster. Over fallen logs, he bounded then splashed through a rocky stream with knee-deep rushing water. More lightning. Jagged spikes of bright white sizzled and struck the earth, then the clouds burst open and hail splattered the ground. Faster, he raced and Ailith burrowed her face into his neck, her breath warm as it washed across his sensitive skin.

"How much farther?" She licked him, actually licked him, her hot tongue stroking across his neck, her divine touch sending a powerful surge of desire bolting straight to his groin.

"Not far." He grunted, his cock hardening again, most

uncomfortably.

Up ahead the tunnel entrance loomed, no more than a ragged path cut through a rocky rise. He slid through a split in the crevice of the wall and plunged into darkness. Water trickled through the cracks in the ceiling above his head and splashed into puddles at his feet, turning the pebbly base into a muddy mess. "Tell me more about the village as it stood in the past."

"In what way?" Her cute freckles stuck out starkly in the cold, her skin chilled and paler.

"I'm aware those from the village are descended from Samuel, the fae king's youngest son, that Samuel became enamored by the village chief's daughter and when the two wed, they created a line of half-blooded fae who remained at the village, but you'll know things our ancient tomes don't hold."

"There are hundreds and hundreds of stories I could tell you that willnae be in those tomes." She pushed her wet hair back from her face and looked deep into his eyes. "You can put me down now."

"I like holding you." He drew in a deep breath, drawing in her exquisite aroma which the wind could never whisk away. "You smell incredible, more fertile than you did this morning. I'm glad we're here, far away from the other unmated males. You'd be driving them insane by now."

"Your advanced sense of smell must be annoying at times."

"I've always appreciated it, actually." His cock jabbed into her bottom as he carried her.

"Hunter!" She gasped his name, her eyes going wide before a glimmer of desire he couldn't miss, lit them from within. "I, ah, please put me down."

"I'll put you down, but only if you promise to walk right beside me along this tunnel."

"I'll walk with you."

"Promise?"

"Murdock had a vision and saw that I willnae be leaving

until you and I have battled, which means I'm eager for a fight."

"I give you my word we can battle, right after I've shown you around the village." Gently, he lowered her to her feet, caught her hand and twined their fingers together. Down the tunnel carved of stone, he guided her, her hand so tiny within his.

"Thank you. What materials did you use for the rebuild?"

"We kept as close as possible to the original mix. Stone and clay for the walls and we topped them with curved timbers to support a thatched roof. The rooms have been furnished with older pieces from the keep which have been set aside for the restoration."

"Wonderful." She stumbled in the dark, and he braced a hand around her waist to keep her upright. "I can barely see the path ahead. Are there any torches we can light to show the way?"

"No, we shifters have exceptional sight and have no issue seeing in the dark." Rubble littered the trail here and there and he made certain she didn't stumble over it by lifting her where needed. "The tunnel thins," he warned her.

"Mayhap I should have mentioned that I'm no' all that fond of extremely tight spaces."

"Why is that?" She seemed unafraid of anything and everything, so prepared to take on even him.

"Once, many centuries ago after my sisters and I celebrated our eighth birthdays together, we decided to take on our first adventure. We'd hiked a full day through the forest surrounding Loch Heart before Cairstine, Lilias, and I stumbled upon a hole in the ground right beside an ancient oak tree. It had the largest trunk and widest boughs I've ever beheld. Fireflies and fairies fluttered all about the foliage and transfixed us."

"Wait, you celebrated your eighth birthdays together? As in you and your sisters are triplets?"

"Aye, we are identical triplets, our features the same,

although Lilias prefers to dye her hair a stunning shade of red. She is such a rebel." She giggled, her body brushing against his in the tight confines of the tunnel.

"I would like to meet them." He wished to know everything about her, for Ailith to share all her childhood memories, just as he wished to share his own with her. "I apologize for interrupting. Continue with your story, your adventure and the fairies."

"Oh, aye, the fairies were so tiny. When I held out my hand, one sat on my palm"—she tapped her palm in the dark—"it stretched out its wee wings and lifted its dainty face to me, all aglow."

"Can you converse with them, the fairies that is?"

"Aye, but only in Gaelic." She rubbed her cheek against his arm as she walked. "Do you speak the old language?"

"All my clansmen do." It was spoken by his elders, and in so doing, ensured each generation came to learn it with ease. "Watch your head through this next part of the tunnel."

"Thank you for the warning." She ducked her head in some places where the ceiling dipped low and so did he. "My sisters and I were always getting into mischief in our younger years, and more so during that adventure since we'd left home without our faerie dust. 'Twas a magical tree, we came to learn, with lush grass and wildflowers surrounding it. Cairstine morphed into a sparrow and flew down the hole and when she returned, she spoke of a deep underground pool she'd found inside, one holding warm water with dozens upon dozens of more fairies fluttering all about it. Well, Lilias and I needed to hear no more. We got onto our bottoms and scuttled down into the hole and whizzed down the chute like on a slide. Once we reached the cavern holding the pool of steamy warm water, we were lost for words. 'Twas just as Cairstine had said. Fairies ducked and dived about, each glowing a soft pastel shade, from pretty pink to pale blue and light yellow. 'Twas as if the fairies had been sprinkled with diamond-dust as well. They sparkled so brilliantly as they played."

"What caused your fear of tight spaces then?"

"Lilias and I couldnae climb out after we left the pool behind, so Cairstine morphed once more into a sparrow and soared up and out of the hole's entrance. She promised to return with Papa as quickly as she could, but unfortunately, she got lost on her way home. 'Twas the next day afore Papa arrived with a knotted rope and dangled it down. He wasnae happy at all that we'd breached the fairies' inner sanctum, not that the fairies had minded. Several had remained with Lilias and me during the night."

"I'd love to have seen those fairies." More thunder, and it shook the ground. Dirt flaked from the ceiling and fluttered free. He held still until all settled, then holding Ailith's hand firmly, he continued along the passageway.

"Are you sure this tunnel is safe?"

"Aye, it's been here for a very long time. Not much farther now, no more than a hundred feet I'd say."

"Then let's hurry." She dug her nails into his palm, her breath fogging from her mouth. "Oh, I see a divide in the tunnel."

"We take the passageway to the left."

"Where does the other tunnel lead?" She gave it a quick glance before continuing with him down the left side of the passageway.

"It veers away inland and comes out several miles to the east of here, quite close to the hills. We'll leave exploring that tunnel for another day." A touch of salt permeated the air, then a rush of fresh sea air breezed through.

"I can smell the loch, and I can see the end of the tunnel." A sliver of light ahead lit her emerald eyes flecked with gold. She dashed past him and clambered up stone stairs leading upward.

"This tunnel comes out right inside the house we've

restored, which we're aware actually belonged to Amelia, another time-walker from the past." He eased around her as she halted on the top step, planted his hands on the trapdoor overhead and heaved. Wood creaked and the trapdoor swung up then clattered back down inside the house. More light filtered through, more fresh sea air too from the open window in the main room.

Ailith scuttled up and twirled around inside the house, her golden ringlets bouncing and the fur hemming her gown leaving a wet streak across the stone floor scattered with fresh rushes. "This is wonderful, and yes, this is Amelia and Olaf's home. It truly is as if I've stepped back in time." She pointed to one wall as he clambered up beside her. "Oh my, you've even restored the stone oven as Amelia had it, and have earthenware pots sitting across the top ledge where she placed them."

"That's Cherub's doing. She ran the final inspection and gave her full approval once done." He eased the trapdoor back over the tunnel.

"'Tis incredible, a job well done." Ailith skipped past a chair tucked under the corner table and halted next to the large oven with its curved arch and peered inside the darkened interior. "Amelia makes the best bannock bread I've ever tasted. I always sit at her dinner table when I visit her."

"Cherub said she and Amelia were close too, like sisters." He strode across to the trunk underneath the narrow open window overlooking the center of the village ruins. Outside, hail pelted the grass and melted within the remains of the fire pit, a deep stone basin which ran a good eight feet wide and fifteen feet long.

"Aye, they are very close and always will be. Amelia is close to me in age, and born in the countryside near my grandfather's castle." Ailith joined him at the open window, a reverent look on her face as she inspected the carved lid of the trunk. "Amelia keeps blankets and plaids in a trunk just like this one, which sits in this exact spot too. Hers holds no such carving inlaid upon its lid though, is instead crafted of reddish-brown wood from a tree Olaf cut down in the forest surrounding the village." She motioned to the pallet in the corner. "That bed is very similar to her son's."

"They have a child?"

"Aye, Joseph. He will turn ten this next summer. He's such a treasure, a child who brings such joy to one and all who meet him. He also holds the skill of foreknowledge, is in fact the first child born to a time-walker, and although no' one of the full-blooded fae, he is still an immortal, his soul having been blood bound to Amelia's through his birth." She heaved up the lid and lifted a plaid from the top of the blankets within, flapped it out and wrapped it around herself. Snuggled within the dry woolen folds, she wriggled her shoulders. "I'm so glad you brought me here."

"There's a fireplace in the bedchamber if you need to warm up. I'll light it now." He motioned to the partially open door at the rear of the main room beyond the small kitchen with its wooden-slabbed benchtop and pots hanging from dangling hooks secured to the ceiling.

"I would love to see the bedchamber."

"It's even furnished. Come with me." He rested a hand at her small of her back and steered her across the main room, pushed the door open and motioned for her to go through first. A large bed with a blue and cream patchwork quilt took pride of place in the room and he passed it then knelt at the hearth. A cane basket was stacked with firewood and he pulled the stringy husk from a log and made a small stack of bark in the pit. From his wrist sheath, he pulled out his dagger and flint, carefully struck the flint then breathed on the sparks and coaxed them into life. Flames flickered and he added wood and brought the fire to a crackling blaze.

Ailith wandered to the side table with its small round mirror propped against the wall and gasped as she caught her reflection. "Ugh, I look like a drowned rat." She picked up the jug and poured water into the matching antique basin, then from the pile of cloths, dipped one into the basin, wrung out the water then chin tipped up, smoothed the damp cloth across her face and neck.

"There's clothing in the ambry if you wish to change out of your damp gown." He picked up the wooden clothes rack propped in the corner and set it in front of the fire. Patting the rungs, he continued, "You can lay your clothes on this rack before the fire to dry. Does that suit?"

"It certainly does since I long to get out of these wet clothes." She eased the blue ambry curtain aside and gently fingered each of the three gowns with a furrowed brow, the first a fine turquoise velvet, the second an emerald satin that matched her eyes to perfection, and the third a royal-blue silk gown with detailed embroidery around the hem and low neckline. A riding habit hung beside the gowns, as well as corseted undergarments.

"Do you see anything you like?"

"Even though I rarely wear gowns, I certainly can appreciate how beautiful these ones are. Still, would there be any men's clothing, a tunic and mayhap a small pair of breeches that I can wear?"

"On the other side of the ambry." He couldn't help but smile, not since his mother had fashioned all the clothing, even hand-stitching the quilted cover gracing the bed. She had the most amazing eye for detail and adored creating clothes from eras gone by. He crossed to Ailith and eyed the shelf holding men's breeches, a tunic, leather jerkin and padded war coat in a tidy pile. "With a sturdy belt, the breeches should stay up."

"I dinnae see a belt."

Neither did he as he searched the shelving. "I'll have to ask my mother to drop one in when she returns from her holiday, for her to add some smaller breeches sized for a woman to the mix here as well."

"Your mother is the seamstress who fashioned these clothes?"

"Aye, she sewed them all by hand."

"She's so clever." She laid a hand on his arm. "Where is she holidaying?"

"Ireland, along with my father. They'll be back in a fortnight. Do you need aid with your laces?" He clenched his fists at his sides, his need to touch her pounding through him. That need stirred his bear and his skin itched again with the demand to shift. His bear wanted his release, to capture some of her undivided attention for himself, to pin her down and claim her, no matter she hadn't yet admitted to a bond forming between them. Aye, with every minute that passed in her company, he became more enamored by her. A bond had certainly formed between them and full moon or not, he intended on proving that point to her.

"I'd appreciate that." She tossed the blanket she'd wrapped around herself onto the bed then gave him her back.

Carefully, he unlaced her stays, the damp velvet separating and her soft creamy skin exposed. She clasped her bodice to her chest as it loosened all the way to her waist then done, he lightly placed his hands on her shoulders, slipped the sleeves to her elbows and turned her around until she faced him. The fire's reddish-orange flames flickered bright and cast a heavenly glow across her high cheeks and the length of her slim neck. Her pulse point thumped and he skimmed the back of his knuckles across the spot. "May I?"

She raised a cautious eyebrow. "May you what?"

"It's best I show you, rather than tell you." Head dipped, he nuzzled her neck and the deep desire to bite her flowed even stronger through him. He pushed her back against the wall and sucked on her neck, his teeth grazing her flesh.

"Hunter?" She moaned his name as she tipped her chin

higher and angled her neck for more of his touch.

"Aye." He plucked her skin with his teeth, so close to biting her, his mouth watering.

"Danger abounds whenever we're alone in a bedchamber together. Have you noticed that?"

"It's a danger I'm becoming quickly addicted to." With one palm sliding around the back of her head, he brought her mouth to his and kissed her. He swept his tongue over hers then delved deeper. More. He needed even more. A surge of desire flooded him and an ache pulsed in his balls as they tightened. All his thoughts scattered as the woman before him let out a low and needy moan.

She rocked her hips against his hips. "This is dangerous territory we enter."

"Not for a mated pair it isn't."

"That's if"—swaying, she wrapped one hand around his neck, her other still clutched in the folds of her bodice—"we're mated."

Chapter 8

Fierce desire rushed through Ailith as she slid her fingers into Hunter's silky black hair and gently dragged her nails over his scalp. All signs pointed to a mated bond forming between them, his decree within her visions that they were soul bound and the sheer magnetism that had drawn them together from the beginning, undeniable. Added to that, she found it immensely annoying how she couldn't halt from touching him.

"You are my chosen one, Ailith." He took one step back, gripped the back of his navy tunic and drew it over his head in one smooth move before letting the cotton slip through his fingers onto the bed beside them. He removed his wrist dagger, set his weapon on the nightstand next to the bed, then unbuckled his sword belt and propped his weapon against the chunky wooden headboard, one carved with the form of the bear. Then ever so gently, he caught her free hand, brought it to his bare chest and let out a savage rumble. "I want you to mark me."

An overwhelming need to do just that roared through her, a need she couldn't fight any longer.

Another fierce rumble vibrated under her palm, his shifter eyes blazing a formidable golden shade and his claws slicing out. "You have until the count of five to do it. One—"

"You are very annoying." She blew out a long breath.

"—two—"

"Extremely annoying."

"—three—"

"Grrr." She flexed her fingers, the light smattering of hair on his chest tickling her fingertips.

"—four—"

"Would you cease counting. I'm getting there." Aggravated, she scraped downward until she reached the waistband of his tan breeches.

He lifted his head and roared. "Give me more."

"Does this hurt?" Five deep gouge lines ran down the length of his chest.

"Nay, and those gouges will heal quickly. I also need to shift. My bear is too close to the surface and since I detest shredding my pants, these have to go too."

"Wait. We cannae both be undressed at the same time."

"Wear my tunic. My shifter blood runs far hotter than a mere human's does and it's already dry." He scooped it from the bed and slipped it over her head.

The fabric, most definitely dry and warm, slithered over her shoulders and rippled to her knees. She stuck her arms down the sleeves, toed off her slippers, wriggled her hips and scooped her gown from the floor. Barefoot, she hopped across to the wooden rack and draped it over one rung.

Thump. One of his boots hit the floor.

Thump. The second.

She faced Hunter with a frown. "I should go while you make the Change."

"No, stay right where you are. If you move beyond my bear's sight right now, he'll chase you. I know he will." His arms rippled with fur as he stepped up to her, his pelt as dark and as silky as the hair on his head. Claws sliced from his fingers and the golden skin of his chest gleamed in the firelight, the marks she'd clawed down the front already gone.

His body was so magnificently male, his hard muscles honed to perfection, with deep grooves framing each of his heavily defined abs. Her toes curled. For centuries, she'd desperately hoped for a mate, and if he was hers, then she could no more leave this chamber than he could.

Slowly, he moved closer, as if he didn't wish to startle her, then he worked the fastening of his breeches loose. "You ready?"

"I've seen plenty of men without their clothing on." She crossed her arms, tapped one foot. "If you must insist on Changing afore me, then strip."

"Who are all these men you've seen without clothing?" He pushed the rawhide past his hips to his feet and tossed them onto the wooden rack beside her gown. His powerful thigh muscles were most impressive, his legs planted wide and his cock waving at her high from within a thatch of dark curls at the apex of his groin.

She hauled her gaze back to his. "Ah, warriors I've trained with. They strut about naked at times, as if I'm no' even there." She maintained her standoff, motioned one hand for him to continue. "I'm waiting. Release your bear."

"You are a very spirited woman. I love that about you." He stepped closer, clasped her face between his hands and brought her mouth closer to his. "Kiss me."

"You're naked."

"Are you scared to kiss a naked man?"

"Never." She'd show him she wasn't. Staring him straight in the eyes, she hooked one hand around the length of his cock and gave it a squeeze. "Where would you like that kiss?"

"I wasn't aware there was an option." He shuddered in her hand, his breath whistling out and his cock stiffening even further.

"You arenae supposed to be enjoying this, Hunter."

Another squeeze.

"You're touching me, intimately. Of course, I'm going to enjoy that." Pressing his forehead against her forehead, he grazed his knuckles along her cheeks. "I need to mark you again."

A long pull of his cock, and another shudder.

"Hell, that feels so good." He clamped his teeth on her lower lip and hissed out another breath as she swept her thumb over the plump head of his cock.

Not on her watch was he marking her again, not right now. She kissed him to keep his mouth on hers rather than biting into her flesh, and he gripped her backside through the thin cotton of his tunic.

"Mine," he rumbled.

"I belong to myself, and no one else." She kissed him deeper, her breasts swelling and her nipples scraping against the cotton of his tunic. His delicious scent was entrenched in the fabric and when she caught another breath, it sent her mind spinning into a frenzy. Heat gathered in her core and flushed between her thighs.

This moment was sublime and she leaned into him, rocked her hips against his hips.

"Ailith, I need to Change, right now." His breath came harder and faster, then he dropped onto all fours and in a fiery display of brilliant lights, bones popped and his bear ripped out of him.

Frustration filled her and she lowered to her knees and wrapped her arms around his furry head. "I hate you, you big oaf."

He stuck his muzzle into her belly, pushed and knocked her over.

"Hunter!" On her back, sprawled on the blue and burgundy mat before the fire, she shoved her elbows underneath her. "What do you think you're doing?"

He stepped in over top of her, his front legs planted either side of her torso and his rear legs either side her thighs. He sniffed the air, his head cocked toward the door as if checking to ensure they remained alone.

"There's no one else here, other than us." She pushed her hands into his thick pelt, right along his belly, his fur a stunning shade of brown, his paws tipped with white and his underbelly a mix of brown and white splotches. She hadn't noticed those splotches before, but then again, she hadn't yet been lying right underneath him.

He grunted, dipped his head and prodded her neck with his wet snout.

"Stop that." She giggled. "I'm ticklish."

His tongue lolled out and he licked across her cheek.

"Hunter, I'm supposed to be getting drier, not wetter." She squirmed about on her back and tried to scuttle out from underneath him, only he stamped his paws on the mat and moved with her. "You're being persistent again." She smoothed her hands along his belly, her fingers sliding through his decadently soft fur. "Let me up."

Another wet lick, across her other cheek this time.

"I said—"

"A third lick, this one swiping across her nose."

"Hunter." She couldn't halt her giggles. "I'm ticklish, remember?"

A fourth lick, along her chin, which made her laugh so hard.

'Twas a shame her chuckles weren't helping to get her stern point across.

A snicker as he pressed one paw over the V-neckline of his shirt, then flicked his claw underneath the navy cotton and sliced down, right between her breasts down to the hem. The sides fell open.

More giggles. She couldn't contain them now, no matter

he'd rendered her as naked as the day she'd been born.

Bright lights shimmered then Hunter was back on his hands and knees over top of her, a lock of his silky dark hair curling across his forehead and a mischievous grin slashing his handsome face. "I love hearing you laugh."

"Your bear is as feisty as you are." She clapped a hand over her mouth to help stifle her laughter, but it didn't help one bit. "You shifted too fast. I was about to ask if your other half would like a tummy rub."

"You were not, but I'll take one anyway." He lowered himself until his belly brushed her belly, then he rubbed gently back and forth, his cheek smooth against her cheek. "You smell exactly like me now."

"Hunter, I may be one of the ancient fae, but I've never been in this kind of position afore, directly underneath a man that is, except for this morning with you."

"I'm not just any man. I'm your mate." He bounded to his feet, scooped her from the mat, and before she could draw a breath, he dropped her lightly onto the bed then loomed over her on his hands and knees again. His heavily muscled body, all firm angles and hot flesh, seared her own. "Ailith, I've waited a lifetime to find you. I want you and my bear wants you and together, we're going to stake our full claim. Are you ready?"

"Nay, I'm nowhere near ready." Although her body screamed differently. Her hands, of their own accord, were already planted on his chest where the smattering of dark hair thinned as it weaved between his defined abs and led downward in a teasing trail before thickening around his stiff cock. She raked down his front, over his trim hips then lifted up and pressed her nose into his neck and drew in his deeply masculine scent, the pine freshness of the forest and the crispness of a salty ocean breeze. He was the only man she'd ever touched in such an intimate way, the only man she ever wanted to touch, and he was right, all signs led toward a mated bond forming between them, but still…they wouldn't have absolute proof until the next full moon rose. "Perhaps we can love each other without fully joining as one?" She wanted to know his touch. She couldn't deny that. "Although this does no' mean you're traveling with me to the past."

"We could love each other without any joining. Whatever you're comfortable with, so am I."

"Aye, for now that is all I'm comfortable with." She wrapped her arms around his neck, his hard body emitting a powerful heat that embedded right into hers. "Give me all that you are, without compromising your choices should we discover that in three weeks, you do in fact belong to another."

"Only those who are mated can abide the touch of another. Never forget that." He pushed his knees between her knees, nudged her legs apart and eased down her body until he lay between her thighs on the bed. Another deep breath as he swirled one finger over her belly and through the golden curls covering her womanhood.

"What are doing?"

"Following my instincts. You smell incredible right now, like a pot of honey. My bear loves dipping his paws into honey. There will only ever be you." He raised her knees, hooked them over his shoulders and touched the tip of his nose to her inner thigh. Flexing his fingers, his claws slicing out then retracting, he growled with a low rumble. "I can't touch my mind to yours like I need to right now. Forge a connection with me through your telepathic skill."

"Of course, allow me." She sought out his mind and swarmed inside as if that was right where she belonged. Tunneling deep, she cemented their link and whispered into his mind, *"I'm here now."*

"I can feel you." He softly nipped her inner thigh, grazed his teeth along her skin then with his wicked gaze on hers, sank his teeth into her flesh and bit down. Not hard, just perfectly

right. *"Marked,"* he murmured, his grin wide, *"and only where a lover could ever mark their other half."*

"Do that again." She stretched languorously, wanting and needing more.

"Now that's what I want to hear." He scraped his teeth along her other thigh, then nipped in a series of small bites all the way to the crease of her groin. Gently, he spread her folds and licked his lips.

"You cannae bite me there."

"I certainly can." He dipped his head, his smile a challenge as he swept his tongue along her slit, and when she lost her grip on the mattress and slithered back down onto her back, he squeezed her nub between his lips and nipped it.

Tingles raced out from that highly sensitive spot and moaning, she rocked her head from side to side. Oh my, perhaps he could bite her there. Hunter laved attention on her, kissing her so intimately below and she thrashed for more. Never in her wildest dreams had she ever imagined the sheer beauty of such an intimate moment. He suckled on her nub and folds, until an ache pulsed between her thighs she couldn't ignore. "I cannae hold on, Hunter."

"Neither can I." He lifted his head and scented the air before diving back in and consuming her.

All her thoughts scattered, every last one.

He kissed her, plucking at her lower folds with his lips, then spearing his tongue deep inside her channel. Heat radiated through her blood and turned her insides into mush. Her heartbeat thumped like thunder in her ears and she needed this, needed him with an intensity that could never be appeased. She pushed her fingers into his hair as he made love to her with his mouth and held on as well as she could.

"Don't come yet, Ailith." He rose, swept his hands over her ribcage and fastened his gaze on her breasts. "I'm not done with you yet." He lunged at her mounds, licked first one puckered nipple then the other before using his teeth and nipping all around her breasts and leaving her flesh dotted with his marks.

Sweet heaven. Never had she known such sheer pleasure as this.

Pressing into his delicious touch, she cupped her breasts and lifted them more fully to his devouring touch. Kisses and bites. She rubbed the achy tips against his teeth and he razzed over both sensitive peaks before drawing one aureole deep inside his mouth. He sucked, hard, his devoted attention making her entire body flood with heat and when he pinched her other nipple, she arched into his body and pleaded for even more.

More, he gave her. Gorging and kissing and licking her breasts, he rolled his tongue around her nipples, then he trailed upward, along the curve of her neck and she stretched her head from side to side so he could cover her neck in delectable bites. Such an intense claiming, one that intensified their need for each other and tugged her heart ever closer toward his.

Her hips swayed into his hips and she clutched his wide shoulders, stroked over his muscled biceps and down his firm forearms as he rose over top of her. So immensely strong and virile. Good grief, she needed to mark him in return, however she could. She raked her nails down his sleek back and tapered waist, gripped his backside—which tightened deliciously in her hands—and dug her fingers into both lower cheeks. She pushed against him with her body and he gave into her demand and rolled over.

She hoisted herself on top of him, straddling his thighs, his shaft rising hot and hard between them. She cupped his balls and his cock lengthened even further, then she dipped her head and licked him with one long teasing stroke from root to tip.

"Ailith, wait. I'll never be able to hold on if you keep touching me like that."

"I need this, Hunter." She settled her lips over the head of his cock and took him deep, just as she'd seen the wenches do when they'd lain with their men.

"Ailith." He shuddered as he gripped her shoulders. "Hell, this is sheer torture. Halt," he croaked.

She sucked harder and he rocked his hips, his cock sliding deeper into her mouth and she took advantage of her heavenly position, gripped the base of his shaft and worked him with her fist as she laved attention on him.

"No more." He jerked out, tipped her onto her back, dived over her and shoved his cock into her hip. He stroked one finger through her heat below before plunging that finger in and rubbing a spot that had her body humming with even more need.

She gasped and bucked against him, his cock pulsing with heat and twitching against her hip bone. She was so slick and close, her soft cries impossible to withhold. Oh, how she wanted him to ground his cock deep inside her instead. "Hunter, I need you."

"I need you too," he murmured against her lips then pushed a second finger inside her.

She screamed his name as she thrashed underneath him, her channel tightening around his fingers and then she was there, soaring free as her inner muscles dragged his fingers deep within her.

"I'm right here with you, Goldilocks." He growled as his seed rushed forth across the bedcovers, then he collapsed on top of her.

Chapter 9

Curled on her side with intense warmth surrounding her, Ailith lifted her heavy eyelids. She blinked and forced the room to cease moving and her vision to clear. Embers glowed in the hearth and through the narrow window at the side of the bedchamber, the sky remained dark, although she sensed the rising sun was near.

"Go back to sleep." Hunter's deep murmur at her back rumbled past her ear, his arm heavy around her waist.

"'Tis almost dawn." The sloshing of waves and the hoot of an owl drifted in from outside. She stretched, her belly rumbling with hunger. Giggling, she covered her middle, not that her hands helped to muffle the noise. "Ignore that."

"I'm hungry too." Hunter tipped her toward him and searched her gaze. "I love sleeping in the same bed as you."

Smiling, she cupped his face and brushed her thumbs over both adorable dimples indented each side of his luscious lips. The enchanting lock of hair curling across his forehead drew her attention too, and she gently tucked it behind his ear, his big body radiating so much warmth. She leaned in closer for a morning kiss then grinned as he kissed her passionately.

He stroked her back, curved his hand over her bare bottom

then lifted her leg and slid it between both of his legs, his crisp leg hairs tickling her sensitive flesh and their bodies aligned perfectly from head to toe. "Good morning," he murmured, in a way that had her melting into him.

"Good morn to you too." She stroked along his stubbly jaw and kissed him again, their next melding of lips bringing such content to her very soul. "It would be a dream to carry your cubs. I want you to know that, no matter what happens in the future."

"It would be a dream to give you one, and I promise you, we'll have a future together, a long and loving one." He brushed his nose through her hair and nuzzled her neck.

"*Ailith, 'tis Cairstine.*" Her sister tapped at her mind along their telepathic link. "*Dinnae get mad.*"

"*What are you doing here?*" She and her sisters all held the same telepathic skill, but 'twas only possible for them to reach each other while in the same time, which meant Cherub must have returned beyond the veil to bring Cairstine through a portal, and all without warning her or taking her back to the past when she did. Aggravated, she muttered, "*Cherub left without me?*"

"Who are you speaking with?" Hunter searched her gaze.

"My sister. She's here."

"Cairstine or Lilias?"

"Cairstine. Give me a moment while I uncover more." She focused again on her sister. "*I needed to leave and Cherub should have warned me she was going.*"

"*You cannae leave yet. Have you forgotten Murdock's vision? Cherub told me all about it. He said you must wait until you and Hunter have fought a battle, one in which you must both undertake to reach a resolution.*"

"*I take it Cherub's told you everything then?*"

"*Aye, she left naught out.*"

"*What about Lilias?*"

"*She remains at the warrior encampment, and I'm now in the guest chamber two doors down the hallway from yours. I packed a bag and brought clothes for us both."*

"Thank you. I've been borrowing things from Isla, but I'm clear out of clothes."

"I need to see you, and afore dawn breaks."

"To feed?"

"Aye."

"I'm at the fae village. Bring me a change of clothes when you come. You can meet Hunter."

"Clothes, of course. Consider it done." Her sister closed their link.

"Cairstine is on her way, and she'll be soaring through the skies to get here fast." She tapped Hunter's nose.

"I wasn't ready yet to leave this bed." He stuck his nose in her hair and sucked on her earlobe.

"Neither was I, but there is no other choice, not with dawn so close."

"Ailith?" A knock rattled the door. "I'm here, with food for you to break your fast as well."

"Wait right there." Her sister had moved fast, and she understood why. She bounded out of bed, nabbed Hunter's shredded tunic from the mat and slipped it on. Holding the flapping sides to her front, she opened the door and accepted the bundle of clothes and boots from her sister, who gave her a sly, wicked smile.

"You are crafty bedding the man already. He must surely be your mate for you to accept him as you have." A light breeze drifted through from the open window in the main room, the odd star still twinkling in the lightening skies.

"The bedding didnae include any completion of the bond."

"So there's no chance you're yet to make me an aunt?" Her sister tried to peer past her into the room, but she closed the door to within an inch and made sure to stand in Cairstine's way. "No possibility whatsoever. We'll be out in just a moment."

"I would say take as much time as you need, but I cannae

risk being caught so far from the keep afore dawn." Still smiling, Cairstine rubbed her hands together. "Lilias is going to be so mad she missed out on seeing this."

"Then dinnae tell her what you've seen." She closed the door in Cairstine's grinning face and walked face-first into Hunter, who'd appeared right in front of her on silent feet. She raked one fingernail down his bare chest and left her stake of claim right there, which settled her a touch. "Dress yourself."

"I want to meet your sister." Possessively, he stroked the mark she'd made on his chest, his gaze locked with hers.

"No' while you're naked."

"Is she well? Her skin appeared rather pale compared to yours, or at least what I saw of her face through the gap in the door."

"She needs to feed and once she has, the rosiness to her cheeks will return."

"Does she travel to this time often?"

"Aye, she finds more acceptance here."

"Why is that?" He strode to the wooden rack, the long length of his back rippling with muscle and his firm buttocks on delicious display. He plucked his tan breeches from one rung and jerked them on before nabbing an inky-black tunic from the ambry and donning it.

"Are you aware of how one with her morphing skill takes their nourishment?" She should dress too. She set the pile of clothes her sister had brought her on the bed, shrugged his tunic off and tugged on a pair of her own skin-tight black leather breeches.

"No, I'm not aware. Tell me." He eased in behind her, smoothed her hair over one shoulder and dropped a kiss on her nape.

"Since their bodies are always reconstructing due to their ability to morph into any creature, whether shrinking to the size of a bat, extending to the width of a dragon, or anything in between, it makes it difficult to eat, so their canine teeth extend and they drink blood, directly from those they choose as their feeders."

"Wait. I do recall learning something like that when I was younger. It's believed that centuries and centuries ago the legend of the vampire might even have first stemmed from a human who met a fae with the skill to morph and wasn't aware of what they truly were."

"Aye, that is quite likely. Usually within all legends, truth exists in some form." Cream tunic tugged over her head and the hem fluttering loose past her bottom, she added a soft leather vest of tan rawhide and strapped her wrist daggers in place and her sword at her hip. Hunter collected his boots and perched on the rumpled blue and cream patchwork quilted bedcovers. He tugged them on and she dropped down next to him, slid her own feet into her calf-high boots and laced them tight.

"Does she feed from you?" A gruff question.

"Aye, and from Lilias too. She is my sister and I would never allow her to perish from lack of sustenance." Teeth gritted, she pushed to her feet.

"Why is it you sound slightly defensive?"

"There are few with her ability beyond the veil, and the fact she drinks blood from her kin, and how she goes about doing so, can cause others to form misjudgment, which I don't appreciate."

"What kind of misjudgment?" His brow drew into a furrowed frown. "There's something I'm missing, but I'm not sure what. Where does she feed from, your neck or your wrist?"

"Primarily the neck. Her bite is sharp at first, then that sharpness disperses as Cairstine releases a substance that allows one to go into a dream-like stance as she feeds. She then heals any incision with a single lick alone. That is a part of her skill."

"During this dream-like stance, are you able to halt her if you need to?" He stood and towered over her, his frown lines deep.

"Nay, she holds the mind of her feeder when she feeds and there is naught I can do to halt her. She could drink me dry if she wished, which is why she only feeds from Lilias and me."

"That sounds dangerous."

"Which is why some say 'tis a dark fae skill she holds. Many will have naught to do with her, even though she is the granddaughter of Ailbert, King of the Fae." She crossed to the wooden drying rack, dug the pouch of faerie dust from the pocket of her gown and hooked it to her belt loop.

"Has she ever taken too much from you or Lilias?"

"Only when she has gone too long between feedings, but you need no' worry over that. Lilias and I can regenerate our lost blood during the deep, rejuvenating sleep of our kind."

"So she can't feed from me if I offered?"

"She could, but only an immortal can survive one of her *ravenous* feedings, and she would never risk one of our half fae-blooded kind by feeding from them." She opened the door and stepped into the main room, her sister's golden spiral curls bobbing loose and long down her back. Very few could tell her apart from Cairstine since they were identical in every way, other than for her sister's currently pale complexion, which gave away the exact depth of her hunger. She pulled her sister into her arms and squeezed her tight, making certain she exposed her neck to her.

Cairstine rubbed her thumb along her jugular and murmured in her ear, "Introduce me to your companion, my dear sister."

"Of course." Releasing her sister, she motioned to Hunter. "Cairstine, meet Hunter. Hunter, this is my nosy sister, Cairstine. I should also warn you, she is like a bloodhound when Lilias and I make new friends. She will wish to know everything about you."

"Aye, I can definitely be a bloodhound." Cairstine eyed

Hunter with fascinated interest. "'Tis lovely to meet you Hunter. My sister has told me so little about you, although Cherub has informed me of a great deal, thankfully."

"Nice to meet you." Hunter eased in behind Ailith, pressed his chest against her back, one hand curling around her waist as he extended his other hand to her sister and shook Cairstine's hand. "When did Cherub collect you?"

"During the dark of the night, right after Murdock had another vision in which he saw the need for me to be here too. I gladly came."

"Interesting." He tightened his hold around Ailith's waist. "My chief's visions are strong. I'm glad you've come."

"I've brought breakfast with me. Sit, and eat." From the countertop, Cairstine handed her a bowl of hot oats and a plate of buttered toast, then picked up a second bowl and plate and handed those dishes to Hunter. With a flourish of one hand, the long, draping sleeve of her red gown swaying, Cairstine gestured to the corner table with four chairs surrounding it. "I've already laid out the cutlery and such."

"How did you manage to bring all this?" Hunter set his food on the table holding a small bowl of honey, jug of milk, two tankards filled with apple cider and a jar of raspberry jam in the center.

"A sprinkle of faerie dust and a simple spell ensured it soared right along with me." Cairstine nudged Ailith with a hand at her back and she crossed to the chair next to Hunter's and sat, while Cairstine sat beside her and picked up the honey and swirled it over top of hers and Hunter's hot oats. Her sister added a splash of milk. "I often long to eat human food. It always looks so delicious."

"You can't even have a mouthful?" Hunter spooned oats into his mouth.

"I can, but I always pay the consequences for it."

"In what way?" Another mouthful, Hunter's interest clearly

piqued.

"My belly aches terribly, and I usually cannae keep the food down for long. I used to have no issue, during my childhood that is, until the age of eight or nine. That's when I began morphing more often, into all manner of creatures, big and small."

Ailith slid a spoonful of oats between her lips and moaned. So divine, the oats exactly what she needed to warm and fill her belly, and to ensure she had enough sustenance to provide for herself and her sister.

Cairstine smiled at her, in that way she always did when slightly amused. "You're a tease."

"I dinnae mean to be."

Her sister rested her elbows on the table and leaned closer to Hunter. "I had an interesting conversation with your clan healer after my arrival, Liam his name was. He said he was well versed in all of the fae skills, even those as ancient and rare as mine. I accompanied him upstairs to his medical rooms and he showed me his meticulously written notes about my ability to morph. He even keeps donated blood from your clan here, in a special refrigerated unit that remains monitored to ensure the temperature of the blood never gets too cold or too hot. In case a blood transfusion or such is needed for one of your kind. He asked if I would like to try one of the bags of blood."

"Did you accept?"

"Nay, that I could never do, no' when Ailith's blood is so delicious." A dark glimmer lit her sister's eyes as she cast her gaze back at her. "Ailith, you have barely touched your food. Keep eating."

She spooned more oats into her mouth, then spread jam over her buttered toast and chewed fast. That dark glimmer always meant the darkness was spreading through her sister, that when she fed, she might very well take too much, and she didn't want Hunter to witness one of Cairstine's *ravenous* feedings, not just yet. 'Twas too soon.

"Drink." Cairstine nudged her tankard toward her. "You need adequate fluids too."

She gulped her cider, her sister's hunger beating at her along their tight sisterly bond.

"Sooo," Cairstine drawled as she cast her gaze back to Hunter. "Murdock tells me you hold the fae tracker skill."

"Aye, I do."

"He also told me of his vision about the battle you and my sister will soon have. I cannae wait to witness that." Her sister dunked one finger into the raspberry jam, gripped Ailith's hand and smeared a small line of red jelly across her inner wrist.

"What battle would that be?" Hunter watched her sister extend one jagged nail and nick her wrist. Her blood pooled, held in place by the jam from running down to her palm. Cairstine licked her lips.

"One fought with swords," Ailith answered Hunter, before sending her sister a frown. "Cairstine, there's no need for this display. I understand you're hungry."

"Your lover needs to know exactly what I am and how tightly you and I are bonded, that I have first right to you."

"I've already explained our bond to him, that I'm one of your feeders, along with Lilias." She pushed her wrist under her sister's nose and Cairstine couldn't withhold her desire. She wrapped her mouth over the blood and licked it away, her saliva sealing the cut swiftly, even though Ailith's own ability to heal would have sealed it within seconds.

"Mmm, I do love an appetizer." Cairstine licked a drop of blood from her lips, her eyes darkening further, no longer emerald, but now a swirling raven color tinged with blood-red.

"I'm done." She polished off her last bite of toast, collected the dirty dishes, carried them to the kitchen counter and stacked them inside the cardboard box on the countertop, which Cairstine must have brought them in. With a pinch of faerie dust from her pouch, she sprinkled it over the box and muttered the spell,

"From whence this box came, swiftly and surely send it winging back."

The box shimmered and disappeared and Hunter raised his brows from the table. "That's impressive."

"Thank you." She crooked a finger at Cairstine and tugged the neckline of her tunic to one side. Cairstine joined her in the kitchen and Hunter scraped his chair back and heaved to his feet.

He stepped directly in behind her, a snarl rattling in his throat.

Cairstine shrugged as if his growl didn't worry her in the least. Likely it shouldn't since she could command his mind as well if she wished to, whether she fed from him or not. A fact she wasn't telling Hunter yet.

"Don't take any more than you should." Hunter gave Cairstine a narrowed look. "My bear will get aggressive if you do."

"Your warning has been noted, and I'll do my best." Her sister's sly smile returned, her canine teeth lengthening and her eyes glowing a deep blood-red, as they always did when the darkness of her need for sustenance swarmed her.

Cairstine opened her mouth and sank her teeth into her neck. No hesitation.

Pain flared then subsided, although instead of sending her into a dream-like state, Cairstine kept her in the present.

Hunter gripped her waist under the loose hem of her tunic, his claws slicing out and digging into her bare flesh. She reached one hand behind her, wrapped it around his neck and drew his mouth to the other side of her neck from where Cairstine gulped blood. "Bite me, Hunter," she demanded. "You'll feel better if you do."

"You're already in pain."

"Your bite always soothes me."

He didn't fight her request for long, giving in fast. He scraped his teeth down her neck, back and forth as he kept one eye on Cairstine on the other side of her, then he did as she'd bid. He sank his teeth into the sensitive spot where her pulse point throbbed then sucked on her flesh, marking her well.

Eyes closed, she swayed back into him, and Cairstine finally relented and released the intoxicating substance that drew her away from her body and allowed her to float in a place where pain couldn't reach her.

She drifted, the man at her back with his mouth on her neck holding her close, and her sister thankfully feeding and replenishing herself as she needed to do to survive. Aye, Cairstine was an immortal, just as she was, but death could come to her sister's very spirit and soul if she chose to forego these feeds and instead become fully dark. If she did, the legend of the vampire wouldn't be a legend anymore. Nay, death and destruction would be set loose on this Earth, and if that happened, even she and Lilias would be unable to halt her.

Long minutes passed, then Cairstine finally released her from her drugged hold, licked across the two puncture wounds and sealed the incisions before stepping back. Her cheeks were flushed a rosy red, her lips coated in blood which she licked away. "You are so tasty, my dear sister."

Hunter continued to hold her back tight to his chest, then he too lifted his head and roared. His bear snapped and snarled in his middle.

"Ah, Cairstine, mayhap you should go." The sky had lightened further, a flush of pink spreading through the deep blue. "Seek your rest for the day."

"Aye, I've fed well." Cairstine morphed into a black-winged bat and screeched as she flew out the open window and soared into the sky.

"She can't walk in daylight?" Hunter asked, his voice all rough and growly.

"She has no' been able to from around the age of nine. That's when she began shifting into so many different creatures.

She chose then to rely solely on blood for sustenance. 'Tis one of the pitfalls of her skill, losing her ability to walk in daylight. She will rest in her bedchamber two doors down from mine at the keep, the curtains drawn. Dinnae fear for her though. She has never succumbed to the burn of daylight thus far and she is rather wise to what she can and cannae do. Once, when she got trapped in the forest as the sun rose, she become a bug and crawled underneath a log to hide from the coming daylight."

"Clever." He traced over the spot where her sister had fed. "How often must she feed?"

"Every few days, although she alternates between Lilias and me so as no' to weaken either of us too greatly." A little dizzy, she gripped the counter as she moved around it toward the door. "I need some fresh air."

"Take my arm." He extended it to her as he opened the door and she accepted his offer and stepped outside as the sun broke the horizon and painted the sky a golden red. Birds chirped in the pines rising high behind the ruins of the village, while in front, waves rolled into shore and splashed the pebbly sand. This land thrummed with enchanted energy, magic belonging to her fae kind.

"I noticed Cairstine's clothes morphed with her." Hunter led her around the stony remains of the central fire pit, through the gap in the crumbled stone of the outer wall and down to the shoreline where the sparkling blue-green waters beckoned her to come and swim. "Mine shred if I don't remove them."

"My sister spells her clothes so when she shifts they travel with her. She learnt that trick as a child." Crouching with one hand on her sword hilt, she laid her other hand on the sacred ground and opened her mind to her skill.

With her inner sight focused on Colin MacKenzie, she allowed her ability to rise and sought what might be awaiting her. She couldn't force a vision to surface, but if one were close to rising, she could nudge it along. Images swirled and she clutched ahold of them.

All around her Colin MacKenzie's warriors slashed their oars into the crashing waves, and Colin MacKenzie himself smirked as he swaggered toward the bow. She was still on board his vessel, and Hunter still lay prone in layers of tartan. Blood seeped around the arrow wound in his chest, the tail end of the arrow snapped off and the head protruding out his side. She couldn't leave him like this, no matter the arrow had already taken his life. Grunting, she tipped him over a little, gripped the blackened arrowhead and heaved. It slid free and she tossed it aside, bound a strip of his ripped tunic around the gaping wound still oozing blood, then settled him back down again.

She'd done this to Hunter, failed him, utterly and completely and now he was dead. Gone from this world. Grief and loss poured through her. She had to maintain her stance, to ensure he never traveled with her into the past. She couldn't fail him again, must heed this vision and the ones that had come before which had shown her his death. She needed to end things between them. No other choice remained.

Carefully, she lifted the folds of the tartan he'd been wrapped in and laid one corner back over his face, while up ahead the MacKenzie's castle rose like a fortress, his stronghold built on an island a stone's throw from the mainland. This was the last place she wished to be. She sniffed, wrapped her arms around Hunter and hugged him close, his presence comforting her even though he was no longer here.

Atop the barbican, a score of guardsmen patrolled in heavy battle attire, their helms covering their faces, and her sorrow slowly subsided as anger took a firm hold. She clenched her fists, her desire to kill throbbing through her.

This was her enemy, and they would perish for taking away her very heart and soul.

Chapter 10

Never had such intense frustration rolled through Hunter as it did in this moment. Ailith was lost within a vision, her eyes glazed and her arms banded tight around something bulky, something she saw and held onto with fierce determination. He crouched in front of her, caught her clenched hands from the air and wrapped them around him instead. She blinked, her gaze clearing and he cupped her face in his hands, his voice a low growl as he demanded, "Tell me what you've just seen."

"Your death still, as I saw in my vision last eve, with an arrow to the chest. I was on board MacKenzie's war galley, holding onto you tight as we sailed toward his stronghold." She stroked one finger along his bottom lip, her cheeks tear-stained. "You need to let me go, Hunter, because if you dinnae, you'll deny us both the chance of a bond should one truly exist. Let me find my way back to you when the time is right."

Aye, he could understand her fears since her visions were a portrayal of the future to come, her combat skill gifting her with the ability to see her enemy's next move, but he couldn't allow her to go into war against their enemy without him. "You ask for too much, Ailith."

"I've traveled often throughout the ages, the entire world

over, and no' once have I ever come across such an obstinate man." She pushed out of his arms and heaved to her feet. Pacing the beach before him, she huffed and puffed and waved her hands about. "Look, last night with you was magical, but whatever has happened between us until now proves naught."

"Don't try to deny our bond exists. We're mated, and you damn well know it." Anger thrummed through him. The full moon had yet to decide their fate, but deep in his heart, he'd already formed an unbreakable bond with her and he wanted more. He wanted to bind them together for all time, for her to accept him at her side, and for her to accept his aid in her duty to her people. Aye, he had no intention of allowing her return to the past, not now he'd finally found her. He tried to draw in a deep, stabilizing breath, but barely managed it. She wished to run, and he sensed that to the depths of his soul. "Ailith, listen to me. I can't protect you if I'm not with you."

"I'm an immortal. I dinnae need your protection, whereas you need my protection until we can join together." She stabbed a finger in his chest. "I have no' been waiting over eight-hundred years to find you, only to lose you afore I even get the chance to truly know you."

"There has to be a way around our current issue."

"The only option is the one I've already given you. You stay, and I leave." Palming the hilt of her sword, she stomped along the beach toward the cliffside trail leading around the bay to Matheson Castle.

"We belong together, and if you dare try to leave me"—he set out after her—"I'll simply hunt you down. That's what I do. I'm a tracker."

"I willnae take any further risks with your life."

"Damn it, Ailith. We need to have an actual conversation about this." Swinging his arms, he jogged in beside her and grasped her arm. "We need to address our issues, not for you to just make the decision for us both."

"I cannae stand by and watch you being killed by my enemy, no' when I have the means to halt your pursuit." Glittery faerie dust got tossed and sprinkled over him. "Hunter Matheson, listen to me well. No longer shall you remember me or any of the time we've spent together, no' one single moment. I shall be as if a stranger to you, an annoying stranger, one you cannae wait to be rid of. Do you understand me?"

"Aye." He pushed the answer from his mouth, the woman before him fluttering in and out of his vision, her words tearing at his very heart. "You're a stranger," he mumbled, fists clenched and his claws slicing out and stabbing into his palms. "An annoying stranger."

"That's right, and now you no longer see me, no' at all." She continued to blur before his eyes as she stepped farther away from him, her voice drifting on the breeze.

"Don't leave me!" He thumped his chest, anguish slashing through him with such fierce intensity, only she was gone…whoever she was.

Someone had been here, then disappeared into thin air.

How the hell had she…she…she…

Who had just been here with him?

He lifted his head, his bear clawing for his release.

The wind rushed up the cliff face and washed over him, bringing with it the salty scent of the sea and the crispness of the Highlands he so adored. This was his home, only something was missing. The lingering scent of strawberries and—he sniffed—was that fertile woman?

Overhead, the heavy boughs of the pines swayed and he dropped to all fours as pain seared through him, his bear ripping free. The Change was fast, far swifter than any Change he'd ever undergone before, and he slapped his paws down on the forest floor and charged into the depths of the forest.

These woods had always brought such calm to his very soul, but not right now. Desperation thrummed through him. He bolted around in circles, thrashing through the underbrush only to end up at the cliff face again, his clothes torn and fluttering away in the wind, his wrist dagger and sword scattered across the path.

He heaved up onto his hind legs and dug his claws into the trunk of a towering tree. Slashing downward, he bellowed and bellowed. Loss, unlike any he'd ever experienced before, pummeled through him.

His thoughts were so jumbled, patches of time missing here and there. He couldn't even recall waking up this morning and leaving the keep, or why he'd headed out here all alone, along the cliff trail toward the ruins of the fae village.

The sun rose higher and he made the Change back, scooped his weapons from the ground and hauled his naked butt back to the castle. Small creatures scuttled away into the underbrush as he stormed past them, clearly sensing the riled predator in their midst.

Through the postern gate, he jogged, then took the side entrance and bounded up the stairs two at a time. Outside Liam's door, he rapped and called out, "It's Hunter."

"Come—"

He shoved the door open and stepped inside Liam's medical room, his kinsman seated behind his desk piled with papers, one brow arched.

"—in."

"Something's wrong with me." He slapped one hand against his chest. "My heart hurts, as if it's been wrenched in two."

"I can take a look at your heart if you like, but first you need to put some pants on. There are spare clothes in the cupboard on your right. Help yourself."

"Thanks." Shoving one hand through his hair, he ignored the cupboard and instead paced the room as he tried to explain all his jumbled thoughts. "I'm missing so many memories, large patches of time.”

“Hunter, your willy is still out.” Liam pushed his chair back, opened the cupboard and tossed him a pair of black jeans and black leather boots. “Put those on. I can’t concentrate otherwise.”

“Fine, I’ll get dressed.” Muttering under his breath, he hauled the jeans on, sat on the wooden-backed chair and laced the boots. “Is it possible,” he muttered through gritted teeth, “for someone to steal another’s memories without their consent?”

“It is if you’ve been around Ailith.” Leaning against the windowsill overlooking the inner courtyard, Liam rolled his blue shirtsleeves to his elbow. “She’s one of the full-blooded fae, Cherub’s niece and sister to Cairstine, who arrived through a portal a few hours ago. They’re identical in appearance, although not with their skills.”

“What skills do they hold?”

“Ailith holds the skill of combat sense, and can receive visions of war before they unfold. She’s also a telepath, as is Cairstine.”

“Tell me more about Cairstine.” More pacing. He couldn’t sit still.

“Cairstine holds the skill of morphing. She and I spoke about her ability not long after she arrived with Cherub. I even brought her here to my rooms and offered her some blood from my stock.” He motioned to his refrigerated unit that kept the temperature of the blood stock within from getting too cold or too hot.

“She drinks blood?”

“Aye, and she can’t walk in the sunlight. After she declined the blood, I showed her around, then before dawn, she morphed into the form of a golden eagle and flew out to visit her sister. She didn’t say where her sister was, so I don’t have that intel, but thirty minutes later she returned as a bat. It was incredible to see.”

"None of this sounds familiar."

"Then a word of warning. Steer well clear of their faerie dust, glittery stuff they keep in a pouch at their hip." Liam eyed him speculatively. "I wasn't in the great hall for breakfast yesterday, but I didn't miss the rumors flying afterward. You stated well and clear for all our clan to hear that Ailith was your mate. You've been gone for over twenty-four hours as well, presumably with her. Does any of that information help? Am I jogging any memories yet?"

"No." But Liam was certainly jogging more of his frustration to rise. "What do Ailith and Cairstine look like?"

"Both of them have blond ringlets and emerald eyes flecked with gold, although Cairstine's eyes can change color. I saw them darken to a raven color with blood-red shimmering through them. That happened when she sighted the blood in the unit, the very second I opened the door." Liam turned at the window and searched the inner bailey. "Come here. Ailith is outside now."

"Where?" He was at Liam's side in a flash.

"Seated on the corner bench under the elm tree. You can't miss her."

He fisted his hands and thumped his knuckles onto the windowsill. No one sat on the corner bench, not a damn soul.

I shall be as if a stranger to you, an annoying stranger, one you cannae wait to be rid of. Do you understand me?

Aye, you're a stranger, an annoying stranger.

That's right, and now you no longer see me, no' at all.

He raked his claws into the stone.

Chapter 11

Within Matheson Castle's gatehouse security control room, Cherub turned from the screen feeding the footage from the camera mounted to the eastern side of the curtain wall and looped her arms around Kirk's neck where she sat on his lap in a padded leather chair. She'd spoken to Ailith on her return and understood her niece's fears regarding her last vision and her decision to spell the removal of Hunter's memories a second time, but there was also Murdock's vision to consider. A battle with swords was yet to occur between Hunter and her niece, one which would lead them to Faodail. She drew in a deep breath and played her fingers through her mate's silky black hair. "I'm worried, Kirk."

"We have to let them find their own way to each other." Kirk spanned his hands around her waist.

"I just wish I knew if those two are truly mated, but as yet I've seen only that she's mated to someone here in this time." She rubbed her cheek against Kirk's cheek, her burgundy skirts brushing her ankles as she lifted her feet and slid deeper into her chosen one's lap. "Do you think they're mated?"

"From what I've seen of Hunter's behavior, his desperate need to keep Ailith at his side, I do believe they're mated.

Sometimes a man knows when he's found his soul bound mate, whether the full moon has arisen or not. Jamie and Bella are a perfect example. Deep in Jamie's heart, he knew Bella was his, had been drawn to her well before her inner bear came of age, and even though he managed to keep his claws off her until the month before she reached full maturity, he still struggled greatly until that time. He even went lone bear to try and force some distance between them, to give her that last month she needed." He kissed her softly, gently, his voice a murmur against her lips as he continued, "Then there's the fact that Hunter has never chased another woman like he's been chasing Ailith. What he's undergoing is the hunt, the chase we men take on in pursuit of our soul bound mate. He won't rest until he makes her his."

"I certainly agree there." Hunter was indeed chasing Ailith, just as the warrior shifters from this clan did when they got within sniffing distance of their chosen ones. She ran one finger down the front of Kirk's chest, coasting over the defined muscles and wicked indents of his rigid abs. "Let's say they are mated, then that means I cannae keep two who are mated apart, no' when their journey in discovering their bond is all about the chase."

"Then we need to make certain Hunter remains alive while that chase continues." Kirk buried his nose in her hair and nipped her earlobe. "I think we can manage that. Don't you?"

"They dinnae call me the Fae Angel of Love and the Guardian of my Earthbound Kind for no reason. I'll make certain he stays alive." She rubbed her bottom into his groin and got rewarded with a fierce growl. "'Tis time for Ailith to experience Faodail, a lucky find, and we need to ensure that happens."

"What's your first plan of attack?"

"They appear ready to battle now, so we'll keep a close eye on them, then I'll return Hunter's memories to him should Ailith no' do so. Two of the immortal fae can play the same game she has instigated." She plucked a pouch from the pocket of her gown, one holding dust then extended her cloaking over them both, and whispered in her mate's ear, "'Tis time to make mischief, Kirk Matheson. What say you?"

"I love the way you think, my elusive imp."

She giggled as he pinched her bottom.

This was a bond she wanted for Ailith and Hunter to hold too, a bond she'd ensure each of the unmated males in this clan had the chance to claim with their own chosen ones. Never would she allow any of her kin to fall afoul of Colin MacKenzie. She'd make certain of it.

Chapter 12

Under the gentle swaying bough of the elm tree on the corner bench, Ailith could barely breathe as Hunter stood bare-chested at Liam's window and glared right at her, not that he could see her, but goodness, it certainly felt as if he could. His frustration and anger pummeled through to her.

Not good.

She heaved to her feet as a loud whistle echoed about the courtyard and a score of men in jeans and belted kilts, their billowy training shirts blowing in the breeze, broke into pairs. They tapped their swords to each other's and swung. Steel clanged loud against steel, and sunlight glinted off their blades as they fought.

Moments later and still shirtless, Hunter bounded out the front door in black jeans that molded his strong thighs and cupped his firm backside. He slammed his weapon into one of the men's, his shoulders and arms bulging so thick and strong as he ruthlessly fought.

She slid her own weapon free and swung it in a wide figure eight as she limbered up.

Hunter battled so close as he forced his opponent away from the others toward her hidden spot. He sniffed the air, dragging in a deep breath then bounded clear of his partner and slammed his blade at her. She shoved her sword high and met his powerful strike. "You're Ailith, I take it?"

"Aye, I am." She heaved away and he canted his head to the side, sniffed again then followed her with one very predatory move. "I've lost patches of time, as if someone has stolen some of my memories. I've heard you're one of the full-blooded fae, Cherub's niece and sister to Cairstine, who arrived through a portal a few hours ago. You're identical in appearance, although not with your skills."

"What skill do I hold?"

"Combat sense. You can receive visions of war before they unfold, and I'm also told you're a telepath, as is your sister."

"You've learnt a great deal since you returned. I had no' expected that." With her knees held loose and feet braced wide apart, her sword ready, she swayed from side to side.

"You also hold faerie dust and I believe you're the one who stole my memories. Liam told me I declared to one and all in the great hall yesterday morning, that you were my mate. Now, I need to know what the hell I've done to annoy you?"

"You willnae give up the chase. There is a war coming, one you cannae be a part of." She moved in a slow circle around him, although he kept sniffing, one ear cocked as he followed her every unseen move.

"You're in heat, and emitting some fierce come-and-get-me pheromones. You smell of strawberries too, ripe and ready to be eaten." Another low growl, his teeth gritted and jaw clenched. "I can also scent my own aroma covering yours. We've had skin to skin contact."

"That's because you willnae let me be." She tried to inflict anger into her tone, but instead her words came out all husky. Drat it all. "Go back to your kinsmen and train with them."

"No." He lunged and she heaved back, but not fast enough. His sword tip sliced across her arm and blood seeped. He sniffed again, fear widening his eyes. "Did I hurt you?"

"Nay. 'Tis only a nick." She clutched her arm, darted farther back, around the bench she'd been sitting on then as soundlessly as she could, she whipped across to the side of the keep and ducked past a high trellis covered in sweet peas which provided shelter for a leafy green vegetable garden. Thankfully, not another of his kinsmen were in sight. She lifted her hand from her arm, her skin already pulling together and the wound closing.

"Ailith?" Footsteps clomped and he rounded the corner. Another sniff and he bore down on her before halting a mere step away. "Removing a man's memories is wrong."

"Protecting a man isnae, and dinnae come any closer." His sense of smell was impeccable, and as soon as she could, she'd toss some dust and remove his ability to smell her as well. She swung and their two blades crashed dead center. "I wish I could be rid of you, Hunter Matheson."

Huffing, she twirled and struck again, her second hit far harder than he'd clearly expected since he had to shove one foot back to brace himself against her strike. Giving him no further leeway, she came at him hard again. She attacked, without holding back.

Aye, 'twas time for the hunter to become the hunted.

Chapter 13

Hunter held his position and maintained his defensive stance. Ailith, his unseen opponent, had goaded and taunted him and he'd had enough. Each time she swung, he caught the whistling of her blade and met her blow, but damn it, he'd much rather be kissing her than fighting her, and that thought somehow didn't shock him. Breathing deep, his advanced shifter hearing attuned to her, he pushed her back then when he had her cornered against the curtain wall, he sheathed his blade, tore hers from her hand and fumbled to find her scabbard. Thankfully, he did, then slid her blade home. With her sleekly muscled body squirming against his, he couldn't hold back his bear. Fur rippled across his chest and down his arms as he pinned her hands to the stone wall high above her head, the rest of her held in place by his body alone.

"Hunter," she yelped. "Dinnae let your bear out."

"It's too late for that." His claws sliced free and she squealed.

"Let go of my hands. I need my dust." She heaved against his chest, somehow slipped free of him and ducked under his arm.

"If you dare remove my memories again, I'll eat you for

dinner." He followed her, the exquisite aroma of a woman in heat—smothered in strawberries and his own scent—drove him to distraction. He shook his head to clear it, raced and tackled her. Together, they rolled across the grass, his hand firm around the back of her head as he kept her safely tucked against him. Tumbling to a slow stop, he came up on top of her, trapping her underneath him with her hands restrained high over her head against the grass. His instincts roared, that her fae dust would allow her to escape him, and that wasn't happening again, not on his watch. "You're my mate," he snapped, those words sounding so very right, "and I intend on claiming you."

"What you are is a big oaf."

"No, what I am is your protector." He claimed her mouth in a savage kiss he couldn't halt. She was his woman and never would he let her go. He swept his tongue inside her mouth and moaned at the delicious taste of her. He nipped her lips, greedily sucked on each one, then only once he felt a little more at ease did he pull back an inch. "Who taught you how to use that sword?"

"My grandfather is Ailbert, King of the Fae, a strong and formidable warrior who wields a lethal blade. From the age of eight, I trained under him. One with my skill, whether male or female, must train as a warrior. Release my hands."

"So you can spell me again? Ha, not happening." He grasped both her wrists under one hand, then patted down her neck, across the neckline of her tunic and down the soft leather of her vest. Once he reached the waistline of her breeches, he smoothed across to her hip. Bingo. One leather pouch. He plucked it free and stuck her coveted fae dust in the pocket of his black jeans. One more kiss to her luscious lips and he smiled. "Now I can release you, or your hands at least."

"You're impossible." She pushed against his chest until she'd gained a couple of inches between them then she groaned and sank back to the ground. Gently, she petted his bare shoulders, which had sprouted with fur, his bear thrumming so close under his skin. "Release your bear if you need to. I understand he's incredibly close to the surface."

"No, he should quieten down now that I've got you this close again." His fur retracted, his claws slicing back in, although he wasn't moving from this spot, not when he still couldn't see her and the chance she might slip out of his hold existed. She also felt incredible against him as she wriggled her back into the grass, her hips rocking against his hips. He pressed a soft kiss to her forehead then each cheek and finally the tip of her nose. "No more spelling the removal of my memories. I also want the ones you've taken away, back again, and that's an order."

"I dinnae deal well with orders." More wriggling.

"So I've noticed." He tipped her head to one side, his mouth watering as he stroked along her unseen neck and settled two fingertips over her rapidly beating pulse.

"Dinnae even think about marking me again."

"I've already marked you?"

"Ah, possibly."

"I wouldn't have marked you unless I believed you were my mate."

"Well, that might be what you believe, but that does no' make it the truth."

"Why do I feel as if we've had this argument before?"

"Because we have." She hooked one leg around the backs of his legs, jerked, and suddenly flipped him over onto his back in a cunning move that had her body now plastered over top of his.

He couldn't let her get the upper hand though, not even for a second. Another flip and he had her back underneath him, then he patted her arms down to her wrists, caught her hands and entwined their fingers.

"Brute." She tried to knee him, but he pinned her knees to

the grass with his own knees.

"You're such an enchantress." Breathing hard, he couldn't withhold his grin. "Do you have any more interesting moves?"

"Of course, and I've had centuries and centuries to perfect those moves."

He held perfectly still as he awaited her next move, only she didn't strike out as he expected, but instead licked his lower lip, the warm swipe of her tongue heating him deep within. His bear growled inside his middle, and he muttered, "You'd better follow that lick up with a kiss." Her breathing became stuttered, and he damn well wished he could see her face. "Kiss me, Ailith."

"Let go of my hands and I will." Softly whispered words, and for some reason he sensed the truth in them.

"Being with you both tears my heart in two and makes me feel complete." He released her hands. "Show me you feel the same way about me."

"You are so annoying." She curled her fingers around the back of his head then drew his mouth down to hers. Another lick, then she moaned. "I'm falling for you, Hunter."

"I have a feeling I've already fallen for you."

"I must ensure your protection. 'Tis the only way you'll survive." She kissed him, deeply and passionately, and his very soul cried out for even more.

He kissed her back, once, twice, then a third sweet, mind-bending kiss before murmuring against her lips the words that rushed forth from deep within his heart. "There'll never be another for me, Ailith, other than you."

Chapter 14

Ailith's ability to continue fighting Hunter had fizzled the moment he'd won their battle and pinned her to the ground. She'd been unable to halt herself from licking his lip and when he'd demanded she follow that move up with a kiss, she'd granted that request. She'd kissed him and he'd wrapped his heat and strength fully around her, his wonderful scent too. "Goodness," she muttered under her breath. "I am such an idiot for remaining nearby after I spelled the removal of your memories and forbid you from seeing me."

"You're not an idiot. You're a woman who needs her mate, even though you wish to run from me." His shifter eyes burned a fearsome golden hue. "Remove the spell which halts me from seeing you, and give me back every memory as well."

"I have a wart on my nose and I'm as ugly as sin. Honestly, you dinnae want to see even an inch of me. Wrinkles everywhere too. I am centuries and centuries old, one of the ancient fae."

"So is Cherub and I'm well aware the ancient fae don't age, not a day past your twentieth year. I'd actually be willing to bet I have more wrinkles than you."

"Would you cease contradicting everything I say. 'Tis most annoying."

"Your kisses are divine, and when you push your breasts against my chest, it makes me so hard. All I want to do right now is strip you down, spread your legs—"

"Hunter!" She slammed a hand over his mouth. "Dinnae say another word."

"—and push my cock"—he mumbled through her fingers—"inside you."

"I'm forbidden from binding a mortal to me, unless there is absolute proof we're soul bound."

"I'll give you that proof right now." He lifted her to her feet as he stood, then carried her to the curtain wall and opened a door she hadn't noticed was there before. He walked inside the darkened depths of a slim-walled chamber with gardening tools secured along one side and sacks of seed and soil piled up on the other. At the end of the area, he lit a lamp sitting on a workbench, opened a hidden door and tugged her into a tunnel leading deep underground.

"Where are you taking me?"

"To my lair, as every bear does when needing time alone with his woman. Faodail."

"Pardon? Did you just say Faodail?"

"Aye, it's a sacred place, my sacred place." He continued down the passageway, his hand tight around hers as he led her down a steep incline.

"Murdock said we'd battle, then you'd lead me to Faodail."

"When did he say that?"

"He had a vision, which he told Cherub about, and 'twas afore we slept together at the village."

"We've slept together?" His voice was all growly and rough, his scowl deep as he frowned at her in the flickering lamplight. "You have a lot of explaining to do, Ailith."

For several minutes, he steered her down the darkened tunnel made of stone and grit, then finally they rounded a corner and she gasped as steam plumed and wafted all around her.

"I cannae believe this is happening, that we're here at Faodail, your lair." She stepped into the warm fog and crunched over white grainy sand. A little farther in and the steam cleared, the depths of a cavern opening before her. A pool of hot water rippled, surrounded by slick black stone walls, with boulders and rocks scattered across the sandy curve of the beach. Farther along the curve, the tunnel continued and daylight shimmered through an opening just beyond a rock wall. The salty scent of the sea wafted through. "We're close to Loch Alsh?"

"Aye, it's only a stone's throw away, but inside this cavern, Faodail, we are all alone." He blew out the lamp and set it on the closest rock before gesturing about the gently lit recesses of what appeared to be heaven on Earth. "Welcome to my lair, Goldilocks."

"Why do you call me that?"

"I have no idea. The name just came out." He tightened his grip on her hand. "Give me back my memories, then I might be able to tell you exactly why I call you Goldilocks, otherwise we'll both remain in the dark."

A giggle resounded, one echoing down the tunnel they'd just traversed—Cherub's unmistakable giggle—then a streak of misty white breezed all about and golden dust floated.

"Cherub!" She tried to duck out of the fall of the dust, only it snagged in her hair. "What are you doing?"

"My dear, Ailith, I'm reversing all your spells over your chosen one. There is a time and place for such use of becoming unseen to another and removing their memories, but this isnae that time." More glittering dust, this time falling over both her and Hunter. "Aye, no more shall you remain unseen to Hunter, and may all his memories of you and your time together return."

"I'm going to pay you back for this." She bounded onto a rock and dived at Cherub's essence, only the streaky mist slipped right through her fingers. She plummeted, landed in Hunter's arms, and he grinned so wickedly. "Ugh, you can clearly see me again. How annoying."

"Aye, and every memory has been returned, including my first meeting with you in the great hall following your arrival with Cherub through a portal. I have it all back, every single conversation, every touch and caress, and every emotional kiss and mark we've both given each other." Gently, he lowered her to her feet, snagged the top tie of her vest, tugged it open and stripped the tan leather down her arms and off. Her cream tunic came next, dropped onto the ground, then he unhooked her sword belt and wrist daggers and set them safely aside. "Would you care for a swim?"

"It does no' appear as if you're giving me much choice."

"I'm not anymore." He lifted her cream tunic over her head, knelt at her feet and slid her boots off then rising, gripped the waistband of her black leather breeches and dispensed with those swiftly, as if he'd been undressing her for years. "Unless you can't swim," he added with a speculative glance.

"I can swim. My youngest sister, Lilias, holds the ability to control the element of water and I'm always dipping and diving about with her in the sea."

"Perfect." He removed his sword belt and dagger, snapped the dome of his black jeans open, unzipped and slid the denim down his legs. The fabric got stuck on his boots, but he pulled them off and once he'd stepped clear of his clothing, he stood before her completely and gloriously naked.

She gulped, her fingers itching to touch him, to smooth across his delectable skin. How frustrating.

"Come, let's continue our argument in the water." He scooped her into his arms, one hand underneath her bare bottom and the other her back. "I also need you to come around to my way of thinking. How might I persuade you, do you think?"

"We have fought over who is right and who is wrong about us being soul bound since the beginning." She wound her arms around his neck as he walked into the pool, and unable to help herself, caressed his skin right over his heart. A soft rumble—perhaps more akin to a purr—vibrated in his chest then rose and escaped his lips. Water lapped her bottom then washed across her middle as he gently lowered her to her feet on the sandy pool floor. Oh goodness. She'd missed his warmth terribly since being denied it. She caught his hands, slid them around her waist and when he stretched his fingers and spanned her bare skin more fully, she softly sighed. "I like it when you touch me, and far too much." She settled her cheek on his chest where the heavy beat of his heart thumped. Such comfort washed through her. "I wish the rising of the full moon was closer."

"We can't wish it to come forward, unfortunately, so let's continue to take it one day at a time. We need to remain together and never apart. That's all I'm asking of you, to listen to my request." The darkened water rippled as he backed her deeper into the water, his gaze sweeping her breasts before she walked farther back and they disappeared under the rising surface. His gaze lifted again to hers, his golden shifter eyes gleaming a molten shade in the cavern lit by the thin stream of sunlight coming from the end of the tunnel near the loch. "I want the right to touch you, Ailith, as freely as any man does with his mate."

"You've already touched all of me."

"There is still more I wish to touch." He covered her midriff with his hands, his fingers brushing the undersides of her breasts. "I want to speak handfast vows with you, in the old way."

"Are you asking for marriage?"

"I am." He cupped her breasts under the water, flicked his thumb over first one nipple then the other, his move sending a bolt of heat shooting straight to her core. "Will you do me the great honor of becoming my wife, Ailith?"

"A handfast is only for a year and a day."

"In three weeks, we'll speak marriage vows, as soon as the full moon has arisen. What do you say?"

"Nay." She desperately wanted to say aye, but that she

couldn't do. Needing a moment to clear her head, she dove and swam underneath the water, a wave rippling outward as she kicked hard for the shore.

Hunter burst from the water behind her, clamped one hand on her ankle and dragged her back to him. He flashed a smile full of challenge, his teeth white and sharp, his claws extended. "Never run from a hungry bear, Goldilocks."

"I wasnae running. I was swimming."

"You do like to argue every point I raise." He carried her to the beach, a happy rumble echoing about the cavern as he laid her down on the wet sand. He eased onto his side next to her, flicked her hair away from her breasts and tweaked her nipple.

A fiery tingle radiated from the sensitive tip and flared outward. Her toes curled at the delicious sensations he always stirred within her, and she clutched his arms, dug her fingers into his skin. "Do you remember now why you call me Goldilocks?"

"Aye, because that first night, I found you asleep in my bed, your golden curls falling across my pillow as you rested."

"I'm still unsure what you mean."

"Have you never heard the tale of Goldilocks and the Three Bears?"

"Nay." Somehow, she'd missed hearing that tale.

"It's about a girl called Goldilocks, with golden ringlets just like yours. She goes for a walk in the woods and comes across a house belonging to three bears, who aren't at home at the time. She partakes of their food, then becomes tired and falls asleep in one of their beds."

"Oh, I see, and you found me sleeping in your bed."

"Aye, with no knowledge of who you were, which is why I named you Goldilocks."

"I see." Smiling, she rubbed her body against his body, drawing his scent back into her skin. She likely shouldn't, but she couldn't help herself.

"I need to touch all of you." He tweaked her other nipple

and more tingles flared.

"You have a way of seducing all rational thought from my head." She pushed his legs apart with her knees and snuck one leg between his legs, his erect cock hot and thick and swollen between them.

"When two people make love, rational thought isn't needed." Pain edged his husky tone. "I'm completely and utterly addicted to you, of being with you and I long to be your lover, in every single way."

"I'm addicted to you too." She swept her hands down his body and wrapped her fingers around his shaft. She stroked him in long pulls, looked deep into his eyes. "I love being this close to you."

"Ailith." He groaned into her neck, pushed her inner thighs farther apart and pushed two fingers deep inside her channel below. He twirled them about until he hit a spot that had her gasping for breath.

A depth of wonder filled her, her love for him swarming her heart and wrenching deep at her soul. She could never lose him, not now, not ever. "Keep touching me."

He hit that same spot again and she gulped air.

"I—I—" More gulping.

"I feel the same way too." He moved onto his hands and knees, lifted her onto her own hands and knees as well, then from behind, gripped her hips and crawled in overtop of her. With his chest to her back and his cock in hand, he rubbed it along her slit. Such excitement bubbled deep inside her and she pressed her bottom back into the cradle of his hips and smiled as he rasped in her ear, "My bear is pushing close to the surface and demanding I take you like this. He wants a primal joining."

Her lashes fluttered down, anticipation and heady desire thrumming strongly through her. "You can take me however you please, but all I ask is that you dinnae take my maidenhead. I willnae remove your choices come the next full moon, no' if you arenae mine."

"Not exactly the answer I wanted, but I'll abide by your decision. You'll remain intact." He reached one hand around her thigh and stroked along her entrance, then caressed her nub as he continued to glide the head of his cock back and forth along her wetness.

She wanted him to surge through her barrier and stake his claim on her, to not miss such a chance of a joining, but…but… Ugh, so many dratted buts. Moaning, she squeezed her eyes shut, reached underneath her and grasped his shaft in her hand. He bucked into her hold, his fingers inside her going deeper. She stroked him harder, just as he stroked her. A sweet pressure built in her core. She wanted him to claim her, in every single way, just as she wanted to claim him in return.

"Hell, you're so wickedly tight." He slid his fingers exquisitely deep then glided deliciously over her nub. "I want to be inside you."

"I want you there too. I truly do, but 'tis too soon." She moved with him as her orgasm continued to build.

"Come for me, Ailith."

"No' without you." Pumping him harder, she balanced on the edge of a cliff she longed to fly from, but only if he could fly right alongside her.

"I can't hold on much longer." He flicked her nub and she soared, her core rippling with wave after wave of mindless bliss, and a kaleidoscope of brilliant colors burst in a beautiful display behind her eyelids. Breathtaking.

Slowly, she came back down and opened her heavy eyes.

Sated and still on her hands and knees, she smiled at him over her shoulder. Sultry steam swirled as Hunter still worked his cock in long pulls, his body a mass of muscle and heat covering her back. "What do you need me to do?"

"Turn over," he demanded. "I want you on your back, right now."

Content and sluggish with her moves, she did as he bid and once she was on her back on the sand, he gripped her knees and thrust them apart. Kneeling between her legs, he searched her gaze as he took himself in hand again and pumped hard. Another fisted pull and he jerked, his seed splashing her folds. His essence flowed over her intimate flesh, then he was there, capturing her mouth with a fierce kiss.

Such intense heat built in her middle once again. More. She needed even more. She grasped his hand and guided two of his wicked fingers inside her. "I love you," she whispered against his lips.

"I love you too," he whispered right back, his fingers going deeper.

Liquid heat surged through her middle and she cried out as she rode another orgasm in a fiery blast. Such pleasure overtook her, and she clung to him, her fingernails digging into his shoulders as she held on. "Hunter, there is no one else for me, other than you. I pray you truly are my mate."

Chapter 15

Misty warm air swirled and Ailith stirred awake. Hunter's scent surrounded her, although not the man himself. She breathed deep, a trace of his scent floating to her on the breeze wafting through from the passageway leading outside the cavern, beyond the rock wall.

She opened her telepathic link and touched his mind, *"Do you care to tell me where you are?"*

Warmth flooded her mind, then his voice, *"The last thing I wished to do was leave you, but it's late and your belly was rumbling. The sun is about to disappear below the horizon, and I'm going to set a snare and catch us a meal for the coming night."*

"You didnae wish to return to the keep?"

"No, I wish for more time alone with you, in my lair."

"Then dinnae take too long." She wished for more time with him too. 'Twas impossible not to. She closed their connection, pushed to her feet on the soft sand and stepped into the warm water of the pool where it lapped gently in and receded. She intended to enjoy this magical place a little longer yet. She waded in then went deeper and dived. Glorious, and so divine. She kicked below the surface, glided right across to the

far side of the cavern then emerged and swam with lazy strokes back to the beach.

Head tipped to the side, she wrung the water from her hair and flapped out her clothing. The leather breeches clung to her damp legs as she pulled them on, the cream tunic sticking to her skin as well, but she'd dry soon enough. Golden dust still sparkled within the grains of sand under her feet. Cherub shouldn't have spelled the return of Hunter's memories the way she had, although she couldn't remain mad at her aunt any longer, not when it truly hadn't been right that she'd been keeping Hunter's memories from him. Still, she and Hunter needed to resolve their issues, which meant finding a way to fix their current dilemma. Only where did she start? Mayhap with her skill and her vision which had first brought her here.

She lowered to a crouch, pressed one hand to the warm sand and sent her senses swirling outward. A vision swirled, a heavy rush of images crashing in and through it the shape of a heavily barred door shimmered through. A cell. No windows, although a candle burned in a holder on the wall, its meager light flickering over the gloomy gray-black stones. A pallet lay in one corner, ratty gray blankets tossed over it and a MacKenzie plaid folded across one end. Cobwebs hung from the ceiling, one draping low over a small side table. In the center of the table sat a trencher with bread, cheeses, nuts and wait, was that salmon and were those sugared plums too?

She strode toward the table, her boots clipping across the dusty, scratched up stone floor. She was still dressed as she had been on board the vessel, in a tunic and black leather pants, her leather vest unlaced and the sides flapping free. She stepped up to the table and prodded the fruit with one finger. 'Twas indeed a sugared plum. She picked up the confection and slipped it between her lips and oh my, it melted in her mouth, so sweetly ripe on her tongue. Her belly rumbled and cramped. Why was she starved of food when a tray overflowing with these kinds of glorious offerings sat right in front of her?

She stalked to the door, pressed her ear against it and waited. Not a single noise filtered through the heavy metal, the door bolted shut. Slamming her fist against it, she yelled, "Is anyone there?"

"Step back, lass." Keys jingled and the lock clicked open. The door swung wide and a massive warrior in a padded leather war coat leered at her through oily black hair falling in stringy locks across his beady gray eyes. Behind him, another candle burned on the blackened wall of the dungeon.

"Where is the slain warrior?" Hunter was gone, never to return, and she sensed that loss to the depths of her heart and soul. "I wish to oversee his burial."

"We tossed him overboard into the mud flats, where he sank into the muck and slime." His evil laughter boomed at her. "He now rests where he belongs, well and truly buried."

She'd done this to Hunter, ensured his death instead of his survival by taking him to the past. She searched outward along her telepathic connection toward Cherub, but got nothing other than an endless black hole. Damn it all. She must be too deep underground to be able to reach her aunt. That could happen if too much rock and metal lay between her and her kin.

"Stand aside, Medrick." MacKenzie issued the order as he stepped through the door, and the man left the cell with a curt nod and a grating thump as he closed the thick panel of steel.

"What do you want from me?" She'd stand her ground, never waver before him.

MacKenzie gripped her sides, gave a shove and sent her slamming back into the wall behind her. She lost her breath, but quickly fought to lug it back in and regain her standing. MacKenzie sauntered across to her, locked his gaze on hers as she planted her feet wide. "I've admired you and your ability to move amongst Gilleoin's warriors for a long time, as if you are one with them, just as any man would be. You're lethal with a blade and can hit a target with your bow and arrow from over a hundred feet distant. You're also one of the full-blooded fae and that makes you a treasure to capture and make mine."

"I belong to no one."

He let off an evil laugh. "Give me your allegiance, and I'll make your days and nights far easier to bear if you do."

"If you dare touch me, I'll slice your head from your shoulders."

"Strong words."

"True words."

"Yet you have no weapon in order to wield that threat."

"Aye, they're missing." She hadn't felt the heaviness of her weapons since being on board his galley. "But you should never underestimate one of the fae."

"I shall take your words under advisement." MacKenzie slid his sword free of his scabbard, shoved her back against the wall and pressed his blade against her throat. In her ear, he muttered, "You show no fear toward me, which I find enticing. I look forward to being able to break you."

"I will never give you what you desire."

"I'll bring a priest here, speak vows with you, and soon you will carry my son and when you do, I'll have ensured the strongest fae blood runs directly through my line."

"I will never consent to being your wife."

He sank his blade even deeper into her neck. Blood trickled, a line that dripped freely, then as he eased his blade back, his mouth curved into a vicious smile as her skin sealed together and healed while he watched with evil fascination. "Aye, you and I shall have fun during your confinement. I shall enjoy bleeding you."

She ducked low, swung one leg out and tried to topple him, only he shoved his blade into her shoulder and she fell, him pinning her to the floor with that blade as he came down hard on top of her. Everything swayed then went dark.

Chapter 16

Hunter strode along the forest trail, his heart full to overflowing with the love he'd been gifted this night. A few minutes ago, the sun had dropped below the horizon and now under the patchy moonlight trickling through the foliage high above, he rummaged within the undergrowth and found a ropy tree root hanging loose from a tree. He looped the ropy root into a noose, gathered twigs and hammered them into the ground and draped the noose over the trap. He knotted the other end to a low branch overhead, tossed a smattering of dry leaves overtop to hide the trap, then along with a wild berry he plucked from a bush, placed it strategically in place as bait. His trap was set.

Shirtless and brushing his hands against his black jeans, he jogged barefoot to the nearest stream winding through their land, knelt at the water's edge and scooped mouthfuls. He and his clansmen always kept supplies in hutches along this river and he climbed the closest tree, hooked one leg over the V dividing the trunk and opened the hutch door. He pulled out a skin, a Matheson plaid and a shirt from within a waterproof pouch, then closed the door.

Gripping the trunk, he slithered back down, dropped onto the leaf strewn ground and noted which hutch he'd need to return to, to ensure it was restocked. Shirt donned and the plaid hooked over his shoulder, he knelt at the water's edge. He filled the skin, attached it to his belt and made his way back along the trail. He collected twigs and the odd log as he wandered along the forest path, then grinned as a soft snap pinged from the location of his trap. Perfect. He tramped back to it, carefully removed the rabbit, skinned and cleaned it beside the stream then returned with his catch and kindling to Faodail.

He bounded into the cavern, set his armful of bracken down next to his woman sitting cross-legged on the sand in her black leather breeches, cream tunic and tan leather vest. Dressed again, her golden locks lying in damp, springy curls down her back, she lifted her emerald gaze to his with something akin to fear flickering within their depths.

"What's wrong?" He dropped onto his knees before her.

"I had another vision, a bad one."

Damn, but he hated her visions, which always seemed to show his death, and which always inevitably left her wanting to run from him. Hopefully though, since she still remained here, that surely meant she'd chosen to talk about her vision rather than running.

"I'll start the fire. I need to keep my hands busy." She moved onto her knees and dug a small pit in the sand, picked up some of the bracken he'd set down and stripped the stringy bark off. She dumped the bark into the pit, then removed her dagger and a piece of flint. She struck the gray rock with her blade. Sparks caught on the bark, and she cupped her hands around the tiny flame and coaxed it into life.

While she added kindling then a log to the fire, he spread his Matheson plaid from his shoulder onto the sand, then worked on creating a spit for the rabbit from some of the sturdier sticks Ailith had left to one side. He poked the rabbit into place and set it to cook over the fire, then eased onto his plaid, his back against the cavern wall.

Ailith crawled into the V of his legs and leaned her back against his chest. "I need this, to feel your warmth surrounding me, to know you're alive and well."

"Tell me what you saw." He unhooked the skin from his belt loop and handed it to her. "Fresh water from the stream."

"Thank you." Stopper unplugged, she brought the mouthpiece to her lips while the fire's golden glow shimmered across her cheeks, then when she'd finished, she handed the skin back, curled into him and snuggled her cheek against his chest. "This last vision followed on from the one afore that. After my capture at the MacKenzie's hands, I no longer found myself on board his war galley with your corpse, but instead restrained in one of his cells deep underground." She cleared her throat, lifted her gaze to his. "The guard told me you'd been tossed overboard into the mud flats, left to sink into the muck and slime."

"I'm not leaving you. We're stronger together than we could ever be apart."

"I couldnae reach Cherub telepathically, which means I'm too deep underground to do so, and from what Colin MacKenzie told me during our conversation, his intention is to speak vows with me, then get me with child. He wants a son who holds the strongest fae blood possible, but I would rather choose death over ever allowing his touch again."

"You're an immortal."

"Aye, which makes it impossible to seek that death."

"We can fix this." Her fear for his safety was something he intended on removing, as soon as he could. He leaned forward and turned the cooking meat over, one arm wrapped around her waist to keep her pinned close. "Your visions are warnings of what is to come, although they are fully interchangeable, correct?"

"Aye, which is why I'm still here and have no' deserted you yet. After the vision, I actually had an idea which might suit us both." She slung one leg over his hips and straddling him, touched her lips to his. "An idea which I wish I'd thought of afore now. Likely the time has no' been right though, but it is now."

"I'm listening."

"You and I shall remain together when we return to the past."

He frowned, canted his head to the side, suspicion rolling through him. There had to be a catch. "Why the sudden change in your position on this? What am I missing?"

"Only those of the full-blooded fae can bind one soul to theirs, that of their soul bound mate. When we join together as one and I speak that spell, you too will be an immortal as I am." She stroked a finger along his lower lip. "So, should you take an arrow to the chest in my coming battle with Colin MacKenzie as I've foreseen, then it willnae take your life."

"You finally believe we're mated?"

"I could continue denying it, but deep in my heart, I know that we are." She lowered her voice to a husky whisper in his ear, then continued, "We shall complete the bond once we're back in the past. 'Twill be best to do so there, where the coming battle is to take place. Our newly forged bond will be at its strongest. Do you agree?"

"Hell, yes."

"Then I shall inform Cherub immediately. We need to leave within the hour."

"Thank you for changing your mind." He gripped the back of her head, tipped it to the side and sank his teeth into her neck. He bit down, so hungry for her, his Goldilocks with her magical fae dust and enchanting charm, her ability to finally listen to her heart too.

Chapter 17

Ailith stood outside the tunnel to Faodail next to the forest of tall pines swaying at the edge of the cliffs. A fresh breeze blew in from over Loch Alsh and stirred the fallen leaves. Hunter paced the trail in front of her, his strong legs pressed against his jeans, his black tunic molding his broad chest and the hem fluttering loose. Every time the wind rose, it lifted the hem just enough to expose the lower set of his rigid abs, and when that happened she caught her breath. He knew why too, since he glanced her way whenever she did, the worry leaving his face for a moment and a sultry smile breaking out.

"How far away are they?" He pulled her pouch of faerie dust from his pocket, strode back and handed it to her. "I almost forgot to give this back to you."

"Thank you, and they're no' far away." She'd detailed her plan to Cherub telepathically, and she and Kirk had agreed that they could now return to the past where they'd complete their bond.

The wind rose again, whipped about overhead and swirled the leaves scattered along the trail. Cherub and Kirk appeared out of the mist with satchels in hand. She bounded across and hugged Cherub. "Hunter is anxious to leave, and so am I."

"We grabbed some things afore we came, which is why we're late." Cherub squeezed her tight in return. "I've updated Cairstine too, and she's going to remain here."

"Lilias is at the encampment, so I will have one of my sisters with me." Since her vision of her and Hunter on board the war galley occurred during the daylight hours, Cairstine would be of little aid. Her sister was already aware of her vision, would be with her in spirit even if not in the flesh.

"For you." Cherub handed her one of the satchels she carried.

"Wonderful. You have my thanks."

"I'll carry it." Hunter plucked her satchel from her hand before she could shoulder it.

"I grabbed some things from your chamber as well." Kirk tossed one of the satchels he held to Hunter.

"Thanks. Much appreciated." Hunter looped both bags over his shoulder, gripped her fingers and murmured, "I'm looking forward to meeting Lilias."

"Lilias finds the waters of Loch Alsh near the encampment rejuvenating. My sisters and I keep tents there."

"I'm glad you're coming with us, Hunter." Cherub squeezed Hunter's arm, her white silk underskirts swishing between the panels of her ivy skirts. Laces bound the sides of her matching ivy bodice together, her ivy sleeves capped over long draping white under-sleeves that reached her wrists.

Ailith leaned her cheek against Cherub's shoulder, drawing in her solid and unwavering strength. She'd always felt more settled when her loved ones were close, and this moment was no exception.

Cherub ran a hand over Ailith's head, her gaze softening. "No mated pair should be separated, no' once they've found each other. Have you forgiven me for my last spell?"

"Aye, of course." She kissed Cherub's cheek and tightened her grip on Hunter's hand.

"We must all remain on high alert while we're at the encampment." Kirk clasped Cherub's hips from behind, the sides of his war coat flapping over his dark pants and sword strapped to his side. "We can't allow the MacKenzie to win any upcoming battle."

"Agreed. Is everyone ready to go?" Cherub extended one arm to Hunter and he grasped ahold of her aunt while she held Cherub's other arm.

"Dinnae let go of Cherub while we travel," Ailith warned him. "Otherwise you'll experience a far rougher journey than you should."

"Will do, Goldilocks."

"Then let's be away." Cherub swirled her fingers through the air and the wind rose and whipped all about. A portal opened and through the dark they soared, while high overhead stars blazed all about.

Lightning flashed within the churning abyss and Ailith's heart lurched as Hunter suddenly pulled her closer and clamped his teeth on her neck. She pressed into him, her head tilted as she gave him what he clearly needed in this moment—to mark her.

She remained close to him through the swirling dark, the heavenly skies lit with stars whizzing by.

Slowly, the whirling wind eased and they bumped down onto soft grass, the forested hills of the Highlands rising high in the moonlit dark. Rolling fields of heather were awash with wildflowers spanning out toward those hills, and before her the jewel blues and greens of Loch Alsh shimmered a darkened hue under the late hour of the night. Along the curve of the bay where the warrior encampment sat, tents dotted the length of the grassy shoreline and flames glowed within the fire pit housed in the center of camp. At least sixty warriors slept around the fire's warmth, the men wrapped in their plaids on the cushioned grass, while four warriors patrolled the shoreline. Others would be keeping a strong guard within the forest, their sentry high in number along their wooded land border with Colin MacKenzie.

Splashing in the loch resounded, about a hundred feet out. More splashing, then a woman emerged from the waist-depth waves closer to shore and skipped out, her dyed red hair a curly wet mess. With her sea-blue tunic dripping water from the hem dangling near her knees, she squealed and ran the remaining distance between them. She got slapped in water and wet skin as Lilias hugged her hard.

"'Tis about time you returned." Lilias pulled Cherub and Kirk in for a wet hug too. "Welcome home, everyone."

"We didnae mean to be gone this long." Cherub kissed Lilias's cheek. "How's the water this night?"

"Beautiful and warm, and difficult to leave." Lilias frowned at Hunter towering over Ailith from behind. "Pray tell, would you be the one called Hunter?"

"You've already heard of me?" Hunter grinned wide.

"Aye, from Cherub when she collected Cairstine. I wished to travel with them to your time, but Murdock's vision didn't include me, so I remained here." Her sister eyed her with a wicked grin. "So, is he your mate then?"

"Aye, he is, and we've come home so I can speak the spell to bind our souls together. 'Twill be best done here since there's a battle to come, and I need our bond ringing at its strongest."

"That is a battle we're all on high alert for. Patrols have doubled everywhere."

"That is good to hear." Cherub cast her gaze between them all. "Although Kirk and I will still speak to the captain and his warriors tonight. We need to ensure a strong battle plan is in place for the days ahead."

"We'll do that right now." Kirk guided Cherub toward the campfire.

"Do you need a plaid?" Hunter removed his from where he'd hooked it over one shoulder and handed it to Lilias.

"I rarely feel the cold due to my skill, but aye, you have my thanks all the same." Her sister tugged the sides of the plaid closer and rubbed her cheek against the warm wool. "Where's Cairstine?"

"Still in Hunter's time. Going off my vision when I awaken on the MacKenzie's vessel, the battle takes place during the daylight hours."

"Oh, I see." Worry flittered across her sister's face, then disappeared and firm resolution remained. "You have no' yet seen the actual battle taking place though?"

"Nay, but now I'm here in this time, I'm certain more will come to me soon. I shall let you know the moment I see anything." She'd alert her sister and aunt as quickly as she could, as she always did when a vision struck.

"Good, although with the hour growing so late, you should rest. 'Tis impossible to miss the dark shadows under your eyes. We'll speak again on the morrow, after you've rested. I'll run another search of this loch afore daylight since that is the route by which you've seen the Mackenzie sail."

"Aye, that would be perfect. Let me know if you see anything."

"I shall. Sleep well, dear sister." Lilias brushed a kiss across her cheek and barefoot, dashed across the grass and ducked into her tent.

She'd need to be in fighting form over the next few days if she wished to pinpoint the exact time of the MacKenzie's coming attack, and sleep was most definitely needed. So was completing the bond, and ensuring it rang at its highest strength. She crossed the short distance to her tent, right alongside her sister's, heaved the thick flap to one side and stepped inside.

All was dark within, the clay lamp sitting on top of the wooden crate in the corner unlit, although she could make out the pile of brown fur pelts she used for her bed with no issue, and no doubt Hunter could too with his advanced shifter sight.

Hunter closed the flap and surveyed her home at the

encampment, one of his brows raised. "I'm glad you like roughing it in a tent."

"I'm a warrior."

"You're also a Princess of the Fae."

"I'm also your mate." Grinning, she crossed to the center pole, kicked off her boots and shimmed out of her black breeches, unlaced her leather vest, removed her weapons and in her cream shirt, crawled under the pelts and into the heavenly warmth of her bed. She stroked her fingers over the soft brown fur as Hunter remained standing just inside the flap. "That was a hint, in case you missed it."

"A hint for what?" A mischievous twinkle lit his eyes as he propped their satchels on the matting next to the pole.

"When two are mated, there are plenty of beddings."

"I would dearly love to bed you, only I can't just yet."

"Do you need to run a perimeter check?" Kirk always needed to upon returning here, to check the scents and sounds about, and to ensure all was well. A shifter thing.

"Aye, because even though I know this land like the back of my hand, we're still in a different time and things will be different. I need to know what fits and what doesn't, both what scents to expect and any changes to the land. That's the only way my bear and I can adequately ensure your protection."

Footsteps clomped outside the tent and Kirk poked his head through the flap. He eyed Hunter. "Do you need to take a run?"

"Absolutely." He pressed a kiss to her forehead, his lips remaining there as Kirk popped his head back out. "I might be a while," he whispered in her ear.

"If I fall asleep, wake me when you return."

"You can be certain I will." With a wink, he snuck out the door.

"*Hunter?*" She squeezed her eyes shut and wriggled within the warmth of the pelts. "*I'll remain in your mind while you run your perimeter check. That way if you encounter any problems, I can come to your aid far quicker."*

"The MacKenzie doesn't strike at night, and I have Kirk with me. He has a vicious bear."

"I can worry if I wish. Whereabouts are you now?"

"We've barely left camp, haven't yet shifted, but we'll be scenting along our land border with Colin MacKenzie's land first."

She pulled the top pelt right up to her nose and followed Hunter's movement. He shucked his clothes and shifted, and she sensed the dual minds within him, of both him and his bear. They were separate, yet also one, his bear's mind as firm and unwavering as Hunter's. His bear wished to scent his surroundings. Track. Then memorize the land and when they came across their kindred Matheson warriors, his bear took another deep breath and committed each man's scent to memory.

"The forest is thicker in this time, Ailith, and rises upward toward the mountains far denser than I expected. There are guards everywhere, thankfully. We're heading back to the loch then we'll track alongside the waterway for a while."

"Be careful as you track." The night wrapped around her as she settled even deeper within his mind.

"I'm a tracker, and I can sense your tiredness along our link. Sleep if you wish."

"I cannae sleep when all I can think about is having your hands and mouth on me. I'm eagerly awaiting that moment." She touched herself between her legs, her body already hot and eager for his touch. She longed for their coming joining, to speak the spell to bind his soul to hers, to ensure he too was an immortal as she was, and to ensure he could never perish at their enemy's hand.

Chapter 18

Perimeter check, aye, done.

Speaking with the warriors around the campfire, aye, done.

His cock still hard at Ailith's last words, aye, aye, and aye.

He jogged back to Ailith's tent, while Kirk disappeared into the lodgings he shared with Cherub across from theirs. He toed off his boots as he entered, shucked his shirt and pants and naked, slid under the covers beside his mate. Her cute nose shone a rosy pink on the end, her cheeks touched with the same color too, and her emerald eyes flecked with gold had gone wide in the near dark as he'd joined her.

"About time you got here," she whispered.

"I sensed you touching yourself along our link." Her sweet curves were all warm, her legs bare and her tunic still donned and keeping him from the skin to skin contact both he and his bear desperately needed. He growled low in his throat, muttered, "I want to strip you off, then I'm going to put my hands and mouth on you."

"Go right ahead."

He didn't need to be told twice. He lifted her tunic over her head and dropped the cotton onto the floor beside them. "Rub yourself against me. I need your scent all over me."

Nipples beading tight, she stroked her breasts back and forth against his chest, the movement like an elixir to his soul. "That better?" she checked.

"It's a good start. Run your hands over my sides and grip my butt."

She brushed her fingers down his sides, right where he'd asked, then clutched his backside and he shuddered from the intense heat she sent surging through him. She cocked a sassy brow and grinned. "Anything else, my big oaf?"

"Cheeky wench." His bear rattled about in his chest. "Tell me the date of your birth. I should know it before I bed you."

"Years pass differently in the land of the fae and we dinnae mark the days as such, but more the seasons or occasions when they fall. My sisters and I were born on the fourth Friday following the sowing of the spring seeds."

"Okay." He mentally calculated a rough date. "So, sometime late March or early April?"

"Aye, around then."

"We should celebrate your birthday on March thirty-first."

"Why is that?"

"'Cause that's my birthday, and we can double up."

"We'd have to quadruple up." She giggled. "I'm a triplet, remember?"

"I haven't forgotten." He rolled her over onto her back, splayed his hands either side of her face on the pelts and trapped her underneath him. Her beautiful eyes glittered in the trace of moonlight filtering through the cream-colored canvas walls. "Scrape your fingernails down my back, hard, extremely hard."

She locked gazes with him, dug her nails into his back then ran them in a gentle, ticklish move downward. "How's that?"

"I said hard."

She giggled again. "'Tis best I dinnae always give into your every request. If I do, I doubt anything good will ever come of it." She tipped her head to the side and tapped her neck. "When you give me your claiming mark, it resonates deep within me. I need another."

"As your claiming mark does with me too." He pushed her knees apart with his own knees, the heat from her entrance washing over his cock, which had gotten even harder since joining her in bed.

"Mmm, I love kissing you." She slid her hands up his chest, speared her fingers into his hair and drew his mouth to hers. She kissed him, then trailed nips along his jaw and down his neck. She nibbled on his sensitive skin where his shoulder and neck met.

He wanted to go up in flames. Every nerve ending exploded with tingling pleasure. "Ailith," he panted, almost lost for breath, "I need to complete the bond with you, right now."

Chapter 19

Ailith rolled her hips against Hunter's as she gripped his hair and tugged on it. "Make us one, Hunter. 'Tis time."

"I crave you." He sucked one of her nipples deep into his mouth and her mind fuzzed.

She wanted him, desperately, particularly since she'd finally accepted that a bond existed between them and she no longer needed the full moon to validate the depth at which it already pulsed. She no longer wished to wait, but to spell his soul to hers and ensure his immediate immortality.

"How do you want to do this?" Golden eyes smoldering, he captured her mouth in a scorching kiss, his big muscled body a fierce heat she wanted to embrace in every way.

"However you desire," she panted, when he allowed her a breath.

"Then hold on tight, because I desire more of you first." He trailed his lips down her body, over her breasts and in a swirl across her belly. He slid down to the end of the pelts, widened her legs and stroked along her inner thighs, his fingers moving along the crease of her groin. Nuzzling her mound, he gathered in a deep breath, spread her legs even wider and revealed all of her to his hungry gaze. "I want my cock inside you, right here,

Ailith." He caressed one finger along her wet slit. "Within the next thirty seconds."

"Agreed." Thirty seconds was all she had, her body so on edge for his. "I'll begin the countdown. Twenty-nine, twenty-eight—"

He blew warm air across her lower folds, his grin wicked.

"—twenty-seven—"

He latched onto her nub and sucked it, hard.

"—twenty-six…" She speared her fingers through his hair and held on. Oh goodness, where was she up to? What an amazing mouth he had. Twenty-something.

A deep probe of his tongue and she exploded, her orgasm shooting through her, then he rose up and whispered, "Twenty-five," and thrust through her barrier and buried himself deep within her.

Back arched, she gasped as a moment of pain washed through her.

"Hell, hell, hell." He gritted his teeth, his body shaking and his head tipped back, the entire length of his neck exposed to her. "Ailith, that feels incredible. You feel incredible around me."

Completely open to him in the way of lovers, she tunneled deep inside his mind, right along the private pathway that already belonged to them. Aye, this was the link she'd created with him before, but now 'twas different. Incredibly different. 'Twas filled with more vibrancy and shine. Brilliant golden filaments lined each side of the pathway of their telepathic connection, which hadn't been there before. Oh goodness. The difference was the merged link of a mated pair, in which he could open the link as well, and not just her. Their joining had enhanced what she'd already created. Heat pulsed in her core and he growled deep in his chest.

She grabbed ahold of his mind and cemented his presence even stronger within her own, then along the link, she murmured, *"Do you see what I see?"*

"Aye, it's the merged link my shifter kind forge with their mate when they join together as one. I could sense it roaring through me when I tore through your barrier." His mind surged so strongly around hers, this private connection between them one that would only ever be theirs. *"You're now mine, in every single way."* He glanced down to where they were joined, lifted up a touch and rubbed his thumb over a smear of blood along her groin. *"Do you feel any pain?"*

"I did, but 'tis receding. Go deeper inside me. That's what I wish for."

"That I can do." He dug his fingers into her waist, his golden shifter eyes blazing in the dark as he thrust deeper, just as she'd asked.

She braced herself against the pelts as he bucked, frantically. Intense heat built in her middle. More heat than ever before. *"Touch me, Hunter."*

He swept one finger over her nub, and sent liquid heat surging through her middle.

She cried out as she rode higher and higher with each of his mind-bending strokes. Such pleasure overtook her, rolling through her in a fiery blast. "I love you, Hunter."

"I love you too." He lunged deep inside her again and again. "You are my everything."

She cried out a second time at their fast joining, wrapped her legs around his legs and stabbed her fingers into his shoulders. She held on as a wave of heat soared through her, another orgasm pummeling through so fast after the first. Breathtaking. He was all hers, forever and always.

"Every inch of me is on fire and burning for even more where we touch." He captured her mouth with his.

She clung to him, her fingernails digging into his flesh.

Over and over, Hunter drove deeply into her and as he did, he licked the skin of her neck then sucked it between his lips. She wanted this, his bite, and to bite him in return, and when he cupped the back of her head and brought her mouth to his neck, her mind whirled into a tailspin.

Rocking underneath him, she couldn't halt her body's need to move as one with him and she scraped her teeth back and forth over his racing pulse point, just as he did the same with her.

"I can't hold on any longer." He bit down and a roaring blast of pleasure consumed her.

Clasping his butt tight, she sank her teeth into him in return and he bellowed and plunged balls-deep inside her, his pace beyond feverish and his thoughts bombarding hers with pure heat and passion. She clamped down on the other side of his neck and marked him a second time, their joining intense and his entire body shaking and making her channel tighten so wickedly. She careened over the edge and soared to the heavens, her inner muscles squeezing and dragging his cock right to her core.

More and more warmth spilled from him and coated her deep within and as it did, she looked deep into his eyes and spoke from her very heart and soul, the spell embedded into their memories at birth. "From this moment forth, I hereby bind Hunter Matheson's soul to mine. Give me a piece of his inner light so that I might guide and watch over him, throughout all of time. He is mine, just as I am his."

A golden glow radiated out from around his body and tendrils separated and floated toward her. She opened her mouth and breathed them inside her body, allowing the merging of all that they were, heart, body, and soul. 'Twas done, a binding of souls that no one could ever tear apart. With tears streaming down her cheeks, her heart so full of new and intense emotions, she murmured, "We are one."

"As we always shall be." He grinned, his golden eyes glowing and his teeth a bright white and looking sharper than ever. He nipped her bottom lip, hard enough to draw blood then he sucked on it until it healed over. He nodded. "I want you to do the same to me."

"Hold still." No hesitation. She bit his lip in return, licked along the bloody, torn edge and smiled as it healed before her eyes, far swifter than his shifter healing could ever do. "Welcome to the immortal world of the fae, Hunter Matheson."

"So, now I'll survive an arrow to the chest?"

"Aye, but I dinnae recommend it, otherwise I will be very angry with you."

"I'll take that into consideration should I see one flying my way." He kissed her again, then closed his eyes and rested his forehead on hers.

Chapter 20

So much heat pounded into Ailith's back as Hunter grumbled before sliding one muscled leg over top of her legs. His purr was loud in her ears, his stubble tickling her cheek and his possessive arm curled around her waist making her pulse race. She wriggled, the tent's pale canvas walls lightening as dawn approached. Goodness, she needed to check for a vision, to get her hand on the soil. She clambered across Hunter's muscled abs, her hand inches from the ground she needed to touch.

"Oomph." He nabbed her around the waist.

"Never mind me," she breezed, almost there, her fingertips grazing the matted flooring.

"Here are the rules going forward." He lifted her back into bed and tucked her underneath him then with one eyebrow cocked, muttered, "I wish to ogle every fine inch of your flesh before you get out of bed in the morning, and by ogle, I mean not while you're trying to escape me."

"Lilias intended on doing another check of the loch afore dawn and I needed to check for a vision. Which means we should probably get dressed and ascertain how things are outside." She heaved one arm far enough out of bed to nab her satchel and drag it back to her. She flipped the top flap back, pulled out a pair of black leather pants, stuck them under the pelt, but got no further as Hunter blocked her path to her legs with his body.

"Reach out to Lilias telepathically, then add me to the mix. We can ascertain how things are going right from this bed."

"All right." She could do that. She touched her mind to her sister's then Cherub's as well, before bringing the three of them together through her telepathic ability and connecting Hunter in too. "*Any updates at present?*" she asked Lilias and Cherub.

"*I'm out in the loch patrolling the waterways as I promised.*" Lilias. "*Tis difficult to see more than a few feet in front of me though. A thick fog rolls in.*"

"*I've done a sweep overhead, and found the mist rather thick as well.*" Cherub. "*The warriors are all on full alert, with men stationed everywhere. Kirk has even sent a team wide, beyond the sentries along our land border with the MacKenzie. He's with them right now.*"

"*Where do you want Hunter and me?*" She pulled a forest-green tunic over her head, but it got caught over Hunter's head as he suctioned his mouth over her nipple.

"*I need you to stay close to camp, where you'll be able to pick up any visions with far more ease.*" Cherub's voice filtered through, strong and firm. "*Report back if you have any. Meanwhile, I'm going to join Kirk on his scouting mission now I've run my aerial check.*"

"*Stay safe, both of you.*" She closed her connection with her kin, her toes curling under the pelt as Hunter continued to suck madly on her breast. She cupped his face in her hands and smiling, lifted his gaze to hers. "I'll never let Colin MacKenzie hurt you."

"Since you're the one who ends up in his dungeons now, in that blackguard's hands, that's my line, not yours." Grinning, he suctioned his mouth back over her nipple, licked and nibbled on it before sweeping to the upper curve of her breast and sinking his teeth in deep. He didn't break her skin, but she wanted him to, her body throbbing everywhere.

Cheeks burning with heat, she pointed at her boots. "You should be helping me dress."

He tapped his chest instead. "Bite me first, same place, then I'll help you get dressed."

"Stubborn mate."

"That is how I'll always be." Tenderly, he palmed the back of her head, brought her mouth to his chest, right over his pec muscle and held perfectly still.

She trailed one finger down his wide chest, slithering in an S shape back and forth over each of his defined abs, then she merged her mind more deeply with his so he could see just how much she loved him. Gripping his shoulders, she ran her tongue over the sharp top edge of her teeth.

"Cease teasing me. Do it, now."

"You are so impatient." Yet she gave in, bit into his flesh and tore his skin. He moaned and rolled his hips against her hips, his cock thick and wonderfully stiff, so she dug her teeth in even deeper.

"I need you. Can't wait." He spread her legs and rubbed his cock along her slit. His look was agonized as he thrust deep inside her, jerked once, twice, three times. His warmth shot to her core in wave after pulsing wave and he mumbled into her hair as he held her tight against him, "Sorry, sorry, sorry. I didn't mean to come like that, but damn it, when you bit me that deeply and strongly, I didn't have a choice."

"I'll have to remember that for the future." She touched the spot where she'd bitten him, the skin already healing and sealing over, just as their immortal kind did. Fisting a hank of his hair, she sank her teeth into his neck this time, and with him still inside her, he got hard all over again and thrust even deeper, his breath jagged and the head of his cock hitting a spot that had her arching her back.

He clenched one hand on her hip, his claws grazing her skin and she broke apart, her channel going tight around his full length. Intense pleasure stormed through her.

He had unleashed her passion so swiftly and she couldn't have fought it either.

To the very stars, she soared.

Slowly, long minutes later, she finally came back down to Earth, and when she did 'twas to find Hunter shimmying her black leather pants up her legs and tucking her tunic in. He tightened the laces of her leather vest, slotted her feet gently into her boots, strapped her daggers to her wrists and fastened her sword belt at her waist before lifting her from the pelts and setting her on her feet. "Promise kept. You're now dressed."

"I love how you keep your promises."

A grin as he foraged through the clothing in the bag Kirk had given him. He donned tan rawhide pants, tugged a tunic over his head and strapped a multitude of weapons to almost every conceivable place on his body. Lastly, he added a cotun and shrugged on his war coat. He appeared every inch a fierce Highland warrior. Her warrior.

She fidgeted with his collar and straightened it, her throat clogged as she tried to push away the emotions suddenly stampeding through her. Never had she had someone like this, who was hers and hers alone, for her to love, to share her life with, and to be loved in return.

Gently, he caught her shaky fingers and pressed them firmly over his heart. "I know. I feel the same way."

"I cannae imagine my life without you in it."

"Thankfully you no longer have to. Let's go before we end up in that bed again." He held out an overcoat studded with bits of steel and she slipped her arms into the sleeves, then ducked out the tent as he lifted the flap for her.

A heavy mist, just as Lilias had said, cloaked the waters, the forest, the tents, and she could barely even make out her hand when she waved it in front of her face. A bird squawked somewhere high overhead, and the crackle of burning logs in the central fire pit, sizzled and popped, the glow naught but a faint orange outline in the heavy fog. "We need to take extra precautions today with this mist."

"It sounds as if Cherub and Kirk already are, your sister and our warrior kin too." Hunter lifted his nose to the air and breathed deep. "I'll stay alert for any unusual scents, while you connect with the land."

"Aye, I will do so now." Lowering to a crouch, she flapped out the tails of her overcoat. Fingers spread, she pressed one hand to the dewy grass. The mist thickened even further and the cold numbed her nose and cheeks. She shivered as images shimmered at the periphery of her vision. "I've got something."

"Keep your mind open to mine. I'm catching the flutter of images just as you are."

"Truly?" Shock coursed through her as he nodded in confirmation. Their mated bond was strong. She opened her mind further to him and he gripped her shoulder where he stood guarding her.

More images swirled, her vision growing in strength.

Two war galleys, shrouded in mist with their sails lowered, sat half-beached on a narrow slice of pebbly shoreline. Dozens of warriors slunk over the bow of one of the vessels and disappeared into the forest. Colin MacKenzie remained at the bow of the second vessel and with one hand raised, gave a silent signal for his men to push them off. Four warriors heaved, then bounded into the galley as it slid back into deeper water.

The water rippled as the vessel glided along the loch, then in the wake of the galley, a seal pup popped its head up. The animal got covered in mist once more and she remained with the MacKenzie. "There's a mist in my vision, just as there's a mist here right now."

"Aye, but there is a mist nearly every morning at this time

of the year. Keep watching," he urged her. "We need more if we're to learn the exact day and time of his strike."

"Agreed." At the bow, Colin MacKenzie stood with his plaid looped over one shoulder, the mist swirling all around him, the war plaits at each side of his head swaying. His men sank their oars into the still waters and heaved. If she could just catch a glimpse of something which would give away enough to determine an exact day and time, then she could halt their enemy before he ever reached their Matheson land.

The mist parted and a golden eagle soared through the skies, the bird her sister's favored form to take, but Cairstine wasn't here and could never fly in the daylight. It wasn't her. Several other smaller birds resting in the rushes alongside the loch cackled and flapped. They heaved out of the rushes and winged away farther down the shoreline then settled again.

More splashing, the seal pup back and now ducking and diving about the rushes as it chased the birds. Slowly, her vision melted away.

"Drat it. I needed more." Gritting her teeth, she stood as a light breeze stirred and lifted the thick mist a touch. She reached out to Lilias again, muttered, *"I have an update. Is all well out on the water still?"*

"Aye, there is naught to report and I am halfway between our encampment and the MacKenzie's stronghold. I'll swim on, right to the fae village. It willnae hurt to check the entire length of Loch Alsh."

"I need you to remain alert for a seal pup, a playful one." She detailed her vision, and her sister murmured her agreement, that they needed more to uncover the exact day and time.

"A seal pup is a good start—wait," Lilias uttered, *"I almost forgot. There's a seal colony near the mouth of the Loch Long, where it meets Loch Alsh. Perhaps a pup has ventured farther from that colony. I'll go in search now afore swimming onto the village. I'll report back with what I find."* Her sister closed their

connection.

Hunter frowned, a fierce scowl deepening his brow. "From your vision, we now know that MacKenzie will attack by both land and sea."

"Aye, particularly since he beached a galley and allowed his men to trek inland. That is in fact a common tactic of his, which is why Cherub and Kirk are running inland checks right now. They're well aware of his tactics."

"We need to warn them both about your latest vision though."

"I'll do so, but first I need a few moments of privacy to tend to my needs." On her toes, she kissed his cheek. "I willnae be long."

"Don't wander too far. I'll alert the warriors to your vision." He stormed into the rising mist toward the central fire pit where the murky outline of two apron-clad women in woolen kirtles became clearer. The women chopped food on a trestle table, the *whack, whack* of their knives on the wooden boards echoing across the clearing. Meat and vegetables got tossed into two large blackened pots sitting on top of the fire. Steam curled into the air, and along with it came the heavenly scent of seafood stew wafting all about. Hunter halted next to Gilleoin's captain and spoke to him.

She needed to hurry. Tugging the edges of her black coat closer together, she ducked into the trees and trekked a hundred feet inland, farther than she would have preferred, but here she could be assured of privacy, the undergrowth thick and lush. Once she'd found a large bush, she crouched behind it then done, wandered toward the secluded pool close by, one she often bathed in once all had quietened within camp.

At the water's edge, she washed her hands and caught the reflection of her messy hair sticking into riotous curls. Not surprising considering the night that had just passed with Hunter. She patted her ever-present pouch of faerie dust. Over the centuries, it had become a necessary part of her arsenal, right along with her daggers and sword. She pinched a little now and sprinkled it over her hair, then along with a quick wish to fix the riot, the air moved and stirred her golden ringlets about.

She leaned over the edge of the pool and smiled as her hair settled back down, nice and tidy once more. If only it were that easy to put the Chief of MacKenzie back in line. He'd been a thorn in clan Matheson's side for a long time, and his desire to hold fae blood in his line, relentless. Over the years, he'd inflicted immense pain to those within the fae village and she didn't doubt he'd continue to do so until he'd gotten what he wanted—the strongest fae blood, that of an immortal's—within his line. Never would that happen though, not on her watch. Nor Cherub or Kirk or her sisters' watches either.

Ambling back through the trees, she connected with Cherub and passed along the information about her vision, then she closed the link as she halted on the edge of the thick line of pines surrounding the encampment. The mist had risen slightly higher again and the grassy trail leading around the sandy shoreline had become fully visible. Tents dotted the area along the curve of the bay and she passed the tent she'd shared with Hunter and trekked toward the center of camp where the fire blazed and their warriors broke their fast. Horses whickered within the makeshift corral to one side and a driver unloaded supplies from a cart and ducked inside the supply tent. Camp life continued on, no matter how close a war could be to breaking out.

Hunter still stood with the captain, his arms crossed over his wide chest as he spoke to him, but when he caught sight of her, he left the warrior's side. She stepped up to him, and he speared his fingers through the long strands of her hair and lifted them to his nose. Breathing deep, he touched his mind to hers, "*I love this merged link of my shifter kind.*"

"*I love it too,*" she whispered to the man who held her very heart and soul in his hands.

"I struggled not to race after you, and I believe I might need counseling on how best to deal with these new and incredibly intense emotions running through me. I couldn't stand having you out of my sight. It was the most difficult ten minutes of my life."

"I'll counsel you. Have no fear there." She grinned and rubbed her body against his, both to soothe his bear since he adored being covered in her scent, and to soothe her own since she too loved being covered in his scent. *"I'm hungry. What about you?"*

"Starved, but not for food." He kissed the top of her head. *"After this battle is done, I want to spend some time alone with you. Just the two of us."*

"That would be a dream."

"Then I'll make sure it happens." He steered her toward a log pulled close to the fire, gestured for her to sit and once she had, he collected two bowls of seafood stew from the cooks and handed one to her as he eased onto the log beside her.

With no spoon, she cupped the wooden bowl and tipped it to her lips. Mmm, fresh fish and a medley of cooked vegetables warmed her belly. 'Twas exactly what she needed. As she finished her meal, a team of men trekked into camp from the woods with a dozen rabbits hanging from a long stick balanced on their shoulders between them.

They lowered their catch to the ground next to the trestle table and with a shout from the elderly cook to a lad of perhaps ten cleaning fish at the water's edge, the boy heaved his pail of fish, climbed the verge and left it with the cook before sitting on a rock and setting to work skinning the rabbits. Hunter stood and added more logs to the fire to keep it ablaze, while the warriors who'd returned dispersed down to the beach, some washing up where the waves lapped into shore, while others rested on rocks protruding along the grassy bank as they partook of their morning meal.

She was here because of these people, to ensure they could continue living off this land, holding this land and ensuring it remained theirs alone. She and her sisters, Cherub and Kirk, would always be here to watch over them, to ensure they were protected and guarded, that they grew from strength to strength, because in the future, the very survival of clan Matheson depended upon what happened here right now.

Needing to shake her mind of all her deep thoughts, she set her bowl in the washtub where two maids scrubbed the dirty dishes, thanked them and wandered along the beach. Hunter, in what she now understood was his tracker-mode, strode along beside her without missing a beat.

"What are you thinking, Goldilocks?" His golden shifter gaze narrowed as he watched her, like a bear about to strike, his attention fully and completely on her.

"Life can be so short for those on Earth. A battle can kill hundreds or thousands of good men, women, and children. I've watched too many battles unfold, but still there are more to come. 'Tis endless."

"You do all you can by tracking your visions with your ability, and fighting the good fight."

"Aye, yet I always wish I could be doing more." She kicked a pebble and it skittered across the shore. "You and I now belong to each other, and all I wish is for all of my fae kind to find their chosen ones and experience such a bond as ours."

"So do I, particularly with Liam and Levi. I want to see them fall as I did. It'll be glorious to watch." He grazed a knuckle across her cheek, stared out across the loch then back at her. "It also scares me to think I could've missed out on being here with you."

"It scares me too. I kept pushing you away rather than pulling you closer, but I have you and your fierce determination, our swordfight and Faodail to thank for our final meeting of minds. I'll certainly be forever grateful to Murdock for his vision which ensured I remained until the right time to leave came to pass."

"As will I. Murdock's always known of my deep desire to have only one person as mine, and I'm glad I've now got you." A slow smile lifted his lips, the same smile now shining bright in his eyes. "I can never go back to how things were before, being alone, even though surrounded by my entire clan. It's time for me to follow my heart and seek out other adventures with you, so from now on, we stick together, for every day that's to come, either here in the past, or far into the future."

"Agreed. I wish to seek out those adventures with you as well." The mist had closed in again, cocooning them within its serene quietness. Goodness, her mate held the most stunning golden eyes, which always followed her every move, the desire within the glittering depths clear to see. He was so tall and solid, a man who held immense love. A confident tracker and a shifter of great ability. His arms flexed against his war coat as the long hem swayed, his sword glinting at his side and the tips of his wrist daggers glinting under his cuffs. He'd altered her from the inside out, from the very first moment they'd met, and she couldn't imagine falling in love with any other man. She grinned giddily as she murmured, "I cannae wait for you to meet my parents. They will adore you, your strength and the love you hold for me and all your kin."

"I'm looking forward to meeting them too, and for you to meet my parents as well. My sister, Bella, is going to love that I've now found my mate." He pulled her into his arms and smothered her in his tight hold.

As the waves washed in with a gentle swish, and the birds nesting in the tall pines chirped cheerily, the harmony of nature's beautiful song all about, soothed her very soul.

She swayed from foot to foot, her eyes closed and cheek pressed to Hunter's chest as she enjoyed the song natured had provided. This moment surpassed any she'd ever experienced here at this encampment and she memorized it. Carefully, she locked it safely away in her heart, to cherish for all time to come.

Chapter 21

Holding Ailith in his arms stirred Hunter's protective desires as nothing else could. He didn't want to move from this spot, could hardly fathom that a battle was on the brink of beginning any day soon. This land was his land, no matter what era in time it was and he would defend it until he no longer could, and with the woman in his arms right at his side. He kissed the tip of Ailith's nose, her cheeks and the corner of her lips. He kissed her softly, reverently, with all the love he held deep within him. "Will you marry me?" he asked in a whisper against her lips.

"Aye," she murmured back, her answer rocking his soul as her mouth melted under his.

She tasted of freedom, of purity and nature, of all his hopes and dreams all fused into one. His inner bear rolled about in his middle, so content and filled with happiness. She was theirs, always theirs.

"Our children," he murmured next, "when we have them, will they be mortal or immortal?"

"I can spell only one soul to mine, being that of my soul bound mate, but all the children I carry will have their very soul entwined with mine in my womb through the natural bond of mother and child. That soul bond can never be severed or broken, so they shall be immortal as I am, and as you now are too." She ran her hand along his bristly jaw. "I expect you to bed me often over the coming days, to give me the greatest chance of conceiving a child while I'm still in heat."

"You can guarantee I'll step up to the mark there." He looked into her beautiful emerald eyes flecked with gold, the mist swirling all about them and tendrils encasing them in a perfect moment of peace and serenity. Wonderful privacy too.

His chosen one held a heart filled with love for her fae kind and he would do his very best to aid her and her sisters, Cherub and Kirk too, each and every day to come, in whatever way they desired it. His duty was now that of guarding and protecting their Earthbound kind, just as it was hers.

He dipped her back in his arms and as she arched and exposed her neck, he pressed his lips right over her throbbing pulse point. She was so graceful and giving, yet held a warrior's heart in that she'd protect her kin in whatever way was needed.

Her eyelids fluttered down and her breath stuttered as he licked her sensitive skin. His jaw ached and his mouth watered with the need to sink his teeth into her. From the very first moment they'd met, he'd wished only to claim her, and he couldn't imagine falling in love with any other woman. She was his one and all, everything he'd ever hoped would be his.

Everything faded away, the mist enveloping them and the fact that they stood on the beach so close to the encampment. It was as if they were all alone in their own world. They weren't though, and he blinked and tried to clear his thoughts. Their warriors were close. Damn, it was a struggle to withhold from loving her whenever he held her in his arms like this.

A twig snapped, somewhere along the fog shrouded tree line, then out on the water a creak and splash traveled to him. His bear roared to the surface and his claws sliced out.

Ailith gripped the front of his padded cotun, her ear cocked to one side. *"Did you hear that?"*

"I did. There's a vessel out on the water and someone lurking within the woods. It could be one of our own men, but then it might not be too."

"My thoughts exactly." She opened a link to her sister, which he caught along their merged connection. *"Lilias, where are you?"*

"I've found a seal pup, a playful one, as well as a galley half beached on the shore. From where I am in the water, I can see two MacKenzie guardsmen on board guarding it."

"There's a vessel out on the water here too, shrouded in mist. I cannae tell the size or who it belongs too, but 'tis almost here and 'twill be making landfall within minutes."

"It has to be Colin MacKenzie. I'll update Cherub and ensure she returns to camp. You deal with the blackguard, and make sure you take him down. I'm on my way back. Hunter?" Lilias questioned him.

"I'm here."

"Take care of my sister."

"You have my word I will."

The battle was about to begin.

A war cry sounded and through the mist a galley appeared. At the helm, the Chief of MacKenzie bellowed an order and his men slashed their oars into the swell and steered it directly toward land. The vessel cut across the rippling waves, the marksmen on board notching their arrows.

"Nay, no' arrows." Ailith grabbed his sleeve. "We have to get out of here now."

"I'm on it." From the misty trees, a huge band of warriors burst out, their MacKenzie plaid clear to see, their shields raised and swords punched high into the air. He always met a battle head on, only right now he and Ailith were trapped between dozens and dozens of enemy warriors and they needed to get out of here and back within the protective circle of their own men.

He slung Ailith over his shoulder and raced back along the beach toward camp.

"Put me down, Hunter. I can run myself." She clutched his pumping arms, her mind still linked with his as she searched the mist behind them for their enemy and sent him the images she caught.

"We have to stay ahead of them. Hold tight, Goldilocks. We need our own men at our back, not the MacKenzies." He picked up his speed, calling on his shifter strength and ability to gain more of a lead. The pebbly shoreline blurred at the swift pace he reached, everything whizzing by.

"I had no idea you could move so fast."

"I can when the need arises." He raced up the grassy verge, their warriors having already heard the MacKenzie clan's war cry. He set Ailith back on her feet and shouted to his kinsmen, "All to arms. We battle this day."

Kirk and Cherub appeared in a rush of wind, Kirk's sword-arm thrust high as he yelled, "We will not fall, nor allow Colin MacKenzie to take our land. It's time to fight, as we always have and always will. Let us take these idiots down."

Cherub rushed toward him and Ailith then gripped her niece's shoulder. "Lilias updated me. We cannae let the MacKenzie get his hands on you or Hunter. Fight within the protection of the warriors here, without separating from them. We must alter your vision, for your joint capture to never occur."

"Agreed." Ailith eyed him. "Be careful during the battle."

"I will. You stay right behind me."

"Here." Kirk tossed him a shield.

He caught it, slid his sword free and stood in front of Ailith, right along the line of Matheson warriors who too had raised their shields and swords. Ahead, out of the mist, their fierce enemy drew down on them.

"We fight, for freedom and for our very survival." Kirk lifted his head and roared, his bear so close to the surface, the same as his was.

Colin MacKenzie landed on the beach and bounded from his vessel, his warriors exploding onto shore as well, their victorious shout echoing all about.

They swarmed forward into Hunter's waiting kinsmen. Warriors clashed, the clang of metal on metal piercing through the mist.

Hunter released his own battle cry and swung.

Never would he allow his enemy to win this war.

It was time to fight.

Chapter 22

Ailith cringed as the explosive battle began. Shouts boomed all around, and swords, battle axes and pikes clashed. A warrior came at Hunter and he blocked the fierce blow, their claymores slamming dead center into each other's. Bloodcurdling battle cries ricocheted all about and Mathesons and MacKenzies fought in a fray of fierce fighting.

"Stay close to me," Kirk yelled to Hunter as the two men fought right in front of her and Cherub. "We're shifters and you and I will be strongest when we fight side by side."

"Hear, hear," Hunter chanted then slashed his blade against his adversary's.

Kirk grunted and with a deadly growl that came straight from his inner bear, met two attackers head on, striking first one and then the other with deadly intent.

Her two kin fought, sweat pouring from their bodies while beside her, Cherub whisked her hands about as she stared up at the misty sky. High above, a furious tunnel of wind swirled, which mixed with a tumultuous mass of dark, seething clouds that blackened the sky. Cherub fought with her element of air and she could be a powerhouse when she did. A storm raged high overhead, just as it raged right here on this land too.

Ailith kept her place as weapons clashed and Colin MacKenzie forced his way through the battling men. Their enemy chief met Hunter head to head. Her mate ducked the MacKenzie's high strike, rammed into Colin with one shoulder and took him down to the ground, although not for long. The MacKenzie bounded back to his feet and struck Hunter across his chest. Breath ragged, Hunter gripped his front, his cotun sliced open but no blood pouring forth and she searched the spot to make sure.

Damn the Chief of MacKenzie. He was bloodthirsty, and she needed to help Hunter halt him in his tracks. Before she could move though, her sword at the ready, another of Colin's warriors came at Hunter from his other side and Hunter shoved his blade high and met the fierce blow. Fighting next to him, Kirk swiped his aggressor then after taking care of their enemy and ensuring he remained down, he bounded to Hunter's side and fought the warrior double-teaming with the MacKenzie against her mate. Hunter turned his full attention on Colin and battled him, landing several hard blows, one after the other then ducked a dagger as it flew from Colin's hand.

"I'm bringing forth a tornado!" Cherub yelled to her over the ruckus. "I need your aid, Ailith."

"Tell me what to do and I'll do it." She couldn't stand just waiting in the wings, watching this war unfold.

"I dinnae wish to harm even one of our warriors with this weapon of destruction." Cherub churned the skies until they blackened the entire skyline, her red woolen skirts swishing about her legs and her white fur cloak flapping back from her shoulders. "Ailith, I need you to use your faerie dust to propel this deadly vortex at the MacKenzies, but no' for it to touch any of our Matheson kin. Can you do that?"

She'd never wielded such a powerful spell before, one that could differentiate between so many men as they fought, but she had to do something, or else they could very well lose this battle.

"You can do this, Ailith," Hunter whispered in her mind as he struck another warrior who'd jumped into his fight with Colin MacKenzie. He brought the warrior down to his knees. *"Use me and my bear's ability to separate my enemy from my kin through his senses alone."* He knocked the warrior out with the hilt of his sword, just as Colin MacKenzie swiped across Hunter's arm. Blood poured from the wound, but it quickly closed over

"Hell, you're one of the immortal fae too." Colin glared at Hunter. "Give me your name."

"You can call me your destroyer, because that's what I'm about to do. Destroy you."

"Look out behind you," she screamed to Hunter as another MacKenzie warrior snuck around behind him.

"Do it, now," Hunter commanded her as he twisted about and met the warrior's strike. *"Reach for my bear. He's waiting to offer you his aid. Take Colin MacKenzie and his men and send them packing."*

"Aye, I will." She hurled her pouch into the vortex Cherub had created, then dug deeper into Hunter's mind and connected directly with his bear. She sought out along his bear's senses, caught the scent of each and every Matheson warrior on the battlefield, each like a beacon of light dotted within the raging storm of the battle. She could taste their scent on her tongue, just as Hunter's bear could, even saw within her mind's eye the depth of brotherhood love which Hunter's bear already held for their kinsmen. She sent that depth of love like an arrow that rebounded off each of her kin and connected them to her like a glittering web, including Hunter, Cherub, and Kirk too. With her voice rising high and the golden dust scattering within the churning tornado, she glared at Colin MacKenzie and yelled, "Beginning with you, this wind shall strike and take you with it, along with each man you're connected to. Those within my protective web shall remain right here with me, without any harm coming to them." To the heavens, she lifted her voice, "Do

it now, and do it fast. See my will done."

The tornado touched the ground and whipped about in a dizzying frenzy, picking up first Colin then each of his warriors in turn, one after another. The vortex sent her enemy whirling high into the air, missing every single Matheson warrior. It carried Colin and his men out over the loch then flattened out and when it did, the Chief of MacKenzie and his men plunged with arms waving madly. They splashed into the loch, went down deep then bobbed back to the surface, eyes wide.

"Board your vessel and dinnae look back," she shouted, her dust fluttering from the skies and glittering across the waves.

"You heard my niece. Be gone with you." Cherub whipped her hand and sent another blast of wind into the vessel, just as Colin and his men boarded it. They tumbled into the hull, drenched as they grabbed their oars and rowed.

"We are clan Matheson, the 'Son of the Bear' and 'Blood of Ailbert, King of the Fae.'" Ailith shoved her sword high in the air and her fellow warriors cheered, the men bruised and battle weary, but their spirits still high and strong. "Never will the Chief of MacKenzie take what is ours. We shall never falter."

Out at sea, the MacKenzie's vessel disappeared into the raging storm, then Lilias splashed through the waist-deep waves and ran out.

Her sister flung herself at her and sent water flying. "We did it. The MacKenzie has been sent packing."

"Did you see the vortex Cherub created?"

"Aye 'twas awe-inspiring."

Grinning, Kirk swamped Cherub in a hug, bent her backward and nipped her ear. "You and Ailith were a sight to behold, my elusive imp."

"So were you and Hunter. You two fought well." Cherub beamed as she eyed Hunter. "Welcome to the immortal world of the fae, Hunter Matheson. May you forever stand strong at your mate's side."

"You can guarantee I will." Hunter sheathed his sword and wrapped Ailith up in his arms. He twirled her about, then captured her lips with his and kissed her fiercely.

She kissed him just as fiercely in return, then sucked on his lower lip before sinking her teeth into it. She marked her chosen one, and she'd continue to do so for all time to come.

Never had she believed such a perfect union with her mate awaited her, his shifter soul fully and completely melding with hers. Together, they'd fought an immense battle, and in the years ahead they'd fight plenty more, but always at each other's sides.

Forever, they'd love one another and keep each other safe.

There could be no other way.

She'd ensure it.

Stay Tuned for a Bonus Scene…

Even though this book is complete, I couldn't help but write a bonus scene with Ailith and Hunter. This scene also gives a little insight into the next book in this series titled, Highlander's Courage.

~ Joanne

Bonus Scene

Twenty-first century, a few days after the battle with the Chief of MacKenzie.

Ailith stood at the darkened window inside Matheson Castle's gatehouse security control room after returning with Hunter to his time through one of Cherub's portals. Cherub and Lilias stood rigidly either side of her, shared tension flickering between all three of them. Not unusual. Ailith was connected to her aunt and sister at the deepest level. Clearing her throat, she muttered, "Cairstine is cutting it fine this morning."

The night skies were lightening, dawn a mere few minutes away and Cairstine had yet to return from her night out exploring the mist-shrouded Highlands farther to the north of this keep.

A quizzical look crossed Lilias's face. "Can I ask exactly why we're all spying on the clan physician while awaiting Cairstine's return? That I dinnae understand."

"We arenae spying." She frowned at her sister, then turned her gaze back on the first-floor window across the other side of the inner courtyard where indeed the Matheson clan physician, Liam Matheson, clasped his hands rigidly behind him as he awaited the moment when Cairstine soared across the pre-dawn skies in her golden eagle form.

"This is called surveillance, important surveillance." Cherub gripped the windowsill, her crimson velvet skirts swishing about her ankles as she focused more fully on Liam. "His concern is clear to see and it worries me. We are used to Cairstine and the way she cuts her return in the mornings to a fine degree, but mayhap we should speak to her about it."

"She's been pushing her boundaries more of late, far beyond the fine degree." Ailith's chest tightened and she rubbed it to ease the discomfort. Cairstine was an immortal, but since the age of eight or nine when she'd foregone all food and relied solely upon feeding from her and Lilias, she'd been forced to give up walking within the sunlight.

"I've noticed that too." Lilias caught her hand and squeezed it.

"I have no desire to see her become one of the Bloodthirsty." If Cairstine ever chose to forego her feeds from her and Lilias, then she could become fully dark and should that happen, death and destruction would be set loose on this Earth. Squeezing Lilias's hand in return, she continued, "Liam is well versed in all of the fae skills, even those as ancient and rare as Cairstine's ability."

"We need to speak to him further about her, to ensure he keeps her under his watch." Stepping away from the window, Lilias cast her gaze on Kirk and Hunter seated across the room. Both men had their undivided attention on the monitors before them, the screens trained on each part of the forest beyond the keep's curtain wall. "Do you see her?" Lilias asked them.

"There's no sign yet." Kirk cast a look at Cherub, his gaze softening. "Come here, my elusive imp. I can sense your worry along our mated bond and I need to soothe it."

"She's my niece. I'll always worry about her." Cherub strode across to Kirk, set her hand in his and peered at the screen over his shoulder while she cuddled against his broad back. In his ear, she uttered, "She is blood of my blood, our bond as strong as that between mates."

"Almost as strong." Kirk lifted Cherub's hand to his lips and kissed her palm. "I hold the other half of your soul, so my bond with you is the strongest of all."

Ailith agreed. No bond could trump that of the soul bond.

Hunter snuck a look at her, his golden shifter gaze smoldering with intensity, his mind merged strongly with hers. *"Should anything happen to you, Goldilocks, I'd never survive it."*

"Neither would I if anything happened to you." She blew him a kiss, her chosen one who'd defied the odds and begun the chase with her before the full moon had even arisen.

Beside her, Lilias walked across to Cherub, a white toweling robe donned over her wet blue tunic worn underneath, her red hair still dripping with water from her pre-dawn swim in the loch. With her sister's advanced eyesight, her ability to see through the murky depths of the darkened waters she adored, Lilias searched the extended range on the monitors as Kirk zoomed each of the cameras farther out.

"Do you see anything, even a speck within the blue?" Kirk asked Lilias.

"Nay, I see naught." Solemn words from her sister.

"I'll reach out to her telepathically, and blast her for worrying us as she has." Ailith had had enough. Her sister would certainly get an earful once she connected with her. Turning back to the window, the sky painted with streaks of red and gold and the sun mere seconds away from rising, she sought out Cairstine. She tunneled her mind toward her sister's link along their telepathic connection. Almost there. She sensed the periphery of her sister's mind, dug deeper and—she crashed into a stone wall of darkness and stumbled back at the brutal blow.

"I've got you." Hunter whipped out of his chair and caught her in his arms. He scooped her close to his chest, their private mated bond at full force and his link with her ensuring he too caught the devastating blow, just as she had.

"What happened?" Lilias was at her side in a flash.

"She has her shields up." Catching her breath, Ailith tried to slow the racing of her heartbeat. "She's never done that to me afore."

Hunter tucked her even closer against his chest. "She's gotten trapped in the forest as the sun rose, even became a bug and crawled underneath a log to hide from the coming daylight. You told me so yourself."

"Aye, that is true." Her sister could be resourceful when needed, and that she'd never forget.

"Look!" A shout from Lilias, her sister shoving the darkened window open. "I see her."

"Are you certain?" Ailith combed the skies, then caught the flapping of an eagle's wings drifting on the air currents. Cairstine skimmed the treetops, breezed over the curtain wall, one wing brushing the sides of the stone crenellation. Her sister dove toward Liam's window, pulled back and dropped onto his windowsill just as the sun speared the sky. The rays hit her sister's wings and smoke billowed, her eagle screeching.

Liam bellowed, his yell echoing across the bailey, but he moved swiftly. He bundled a plaid over Cairstine and hauled her into his chamber, then flung the heavy drapes across his window.

"She's safe." She sagged in Hunter's arms. "That was far too close for my comfort."

"Mine as well." He pressed his soft lips against hers, his kiss lifting the chill that had taken her. "We can speak to her later."

"Aye, we can and we will." Immense relief flooded through her. For now, her sister was safe and well in the physician's rooms where if she'd suffered any terribly injury from any burn from the sun, her immortal healing would set in and mend her wounds. Across the room, Cherub eased onto Kirk's lap and snuggled her cheek against his cheek, while Kirk held her tight in his arms and brushed a kiss over the top of her head. Next to her, Lilias closed the window and sagged her forehead against the cool glass. Aye, relief washed through them all, and she didn't doubt they'd all blast Cairstine when they next saw her. Looking once more into her mate's eyes, she murmured, "I need a moment alone with you."

"As I do with you." Without hesitation, he carried her out the door and onto the stone walkway running along the battlements. He rounded a corner, set her down on her feet and pressed her into the early morning shadows still clinging to the wall where the surveillance cameras couldn't quite reach. "We'll keep her safe," he promised, his word once given, never taken back.

"Aye, we will." She'd never allow her sister to choose any other path, other than life. "Please, I need you right now."

"As I need you." Gaze devouring, he took her cheeks in his hands and covered her mouth with his, his body a wall of heat which instantly surrounded her.

"I also need to feel your skin against my skin." A husky demand she couldn't help but issue.

"Toss some dust, and I'll make that happen, right this very second." More of his wickedly muscled body pressed against hers, one hand sliding under the hem of her white tunic, his warm fingers closing in over her breast. Tingles tightened her nipples and doubled her need.

"Thank heavens I've replenished my supply since the battle with the Chief of MacKenzie." She threw a sprinkle into the air and as the gold dust settled over them, she whispered the words needed to cloak them both from sight, then with her fierce need for him becoming an unstoppable beat, she gave herself over to their love and embraced her mate. He made exquisite love to her, with the sun shining down upon them and his glorious body joined fully with hers.

This was the soul bond, a force of nature none could ever deny.

She wouldn't wish to either.

Author's Note

Clan Matheson descends from a twelfth century man called Gilleoin, a man who was believed to have been from the ancient Royal House of Lorne. The name Matheson has been attributed to the Gaelic words Mic Mhathghamhuim which means "Son of the Bear," and the clan chief's arms carry two bears as supporters. In the twelfth century, clan Matheson settled around the area of Loch Alsh, Loch Carron, and Kintail, and gave their allegiance to clan MacDonald whose chiefs were the Lords of the Isles. Clan Matheson became a large and powerful clan with a force of around two-thousand men, although by the middle of the sixteenth century they'd diminished greatly in size and influence due to the blood feuds raging across the isles at that time. This warring left them to possess less than a third of the original Matheson property on Loch Alsh.

It's time for the whispers to reignite. Clan Matheson are the "Son of the Bear."

This story is woven with as much accuracy to the period and locations as possible, although any mistakes made are mine alone. Please feel free to search for any of my other works. I simply adore strong heroines, and have a ton of fun matching them with their honorable alpha heroes.

Highlander's Courage

~COMING NEXT~

The Matheson Brothers, Book Twelve

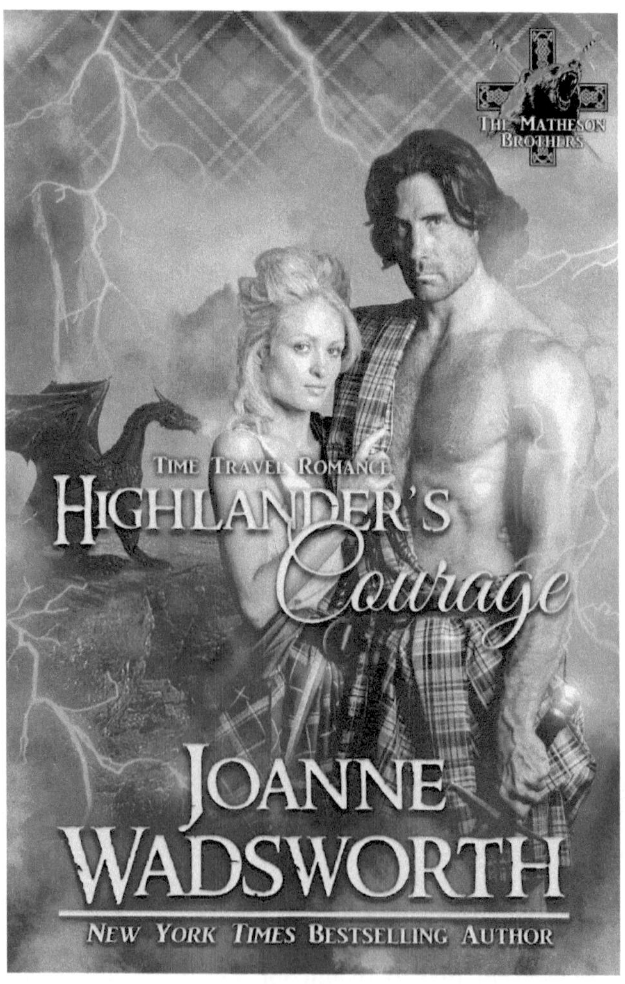

The Matheson Brothers

Highlander's Desire, Book One
Highlander's Passion, Book Two
Highlander's Seduction, Book Three

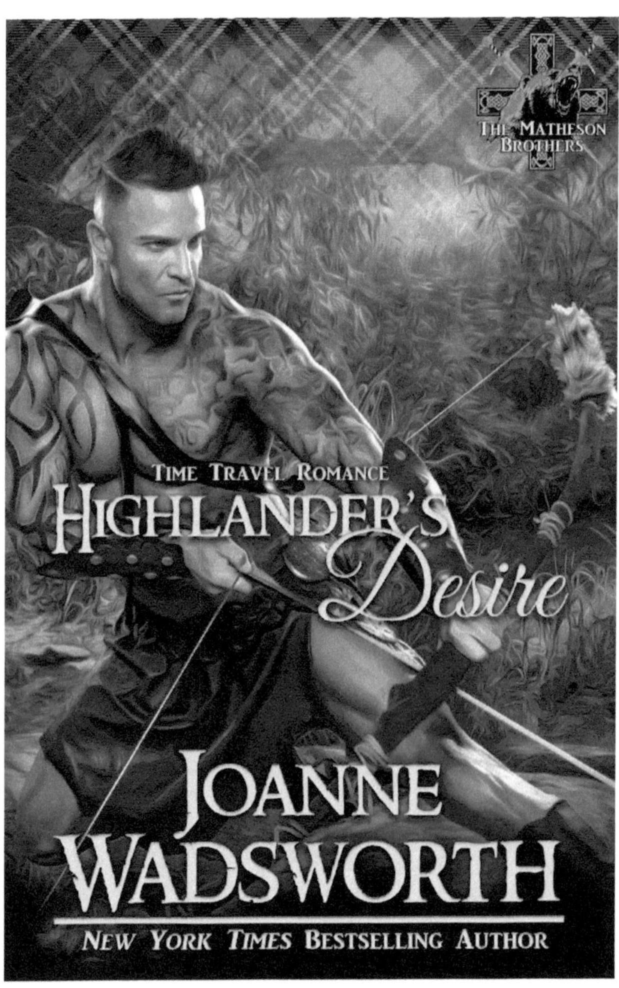

The Matheson Brothers Continued

Highlander's Bride, Book Seven
Highlander's Caress, Book Eight
Highlander's Touch, Book Nine

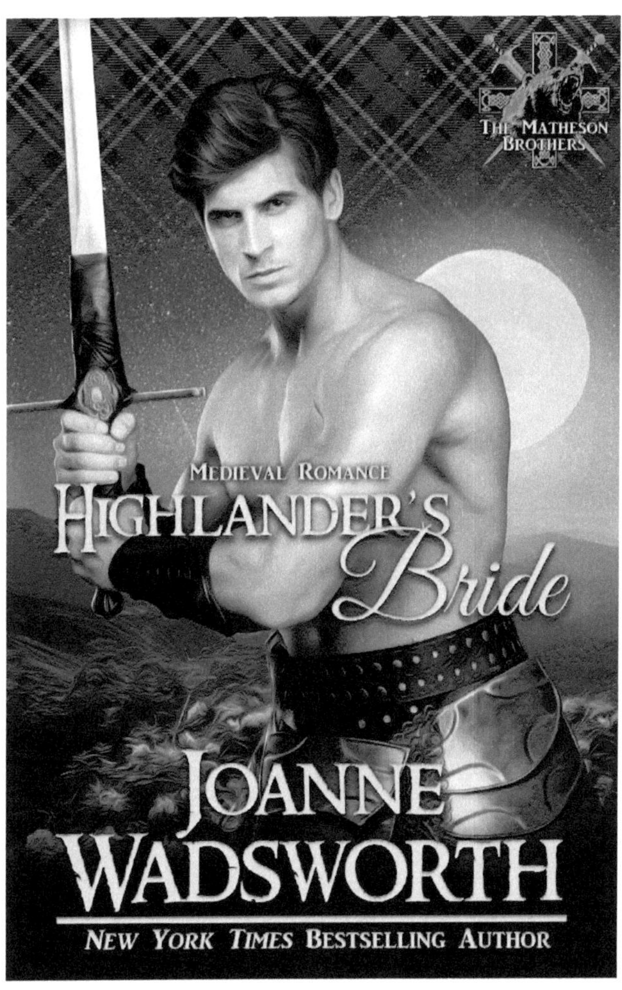

The Matheson Brothers Continued

Highlander's Shifter, Book Ten
Highlander's Claim, Book Eleven
Highlander's Courage, Book Twelve
Highlander's Mermaid, Book Thirteen

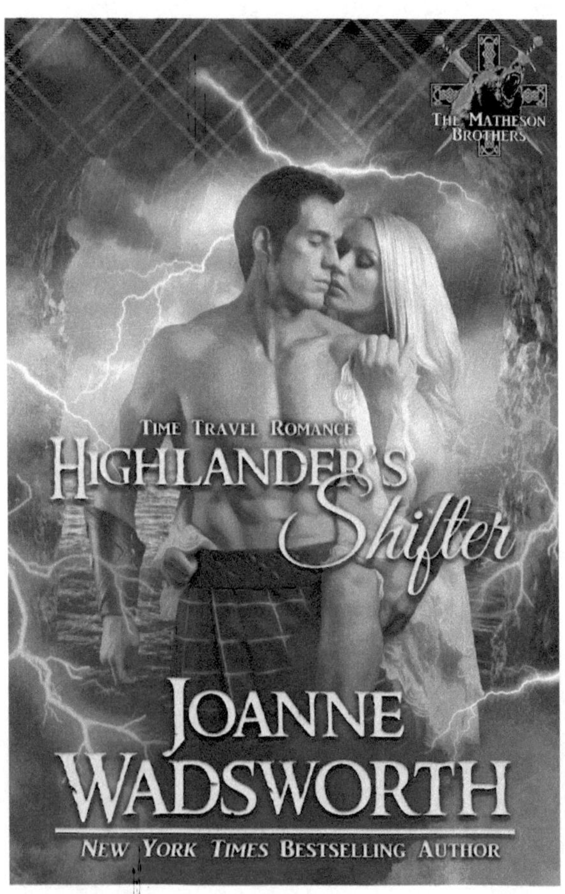

Highlander Heat

Highlander's Castle, Book One
Highlander's Magic, Book Two
Highlander's Charm, Book Three
Highlander's Guardian, Book Four
Highlander's Faerie, Book Five
Highlander's Champion, Book Six

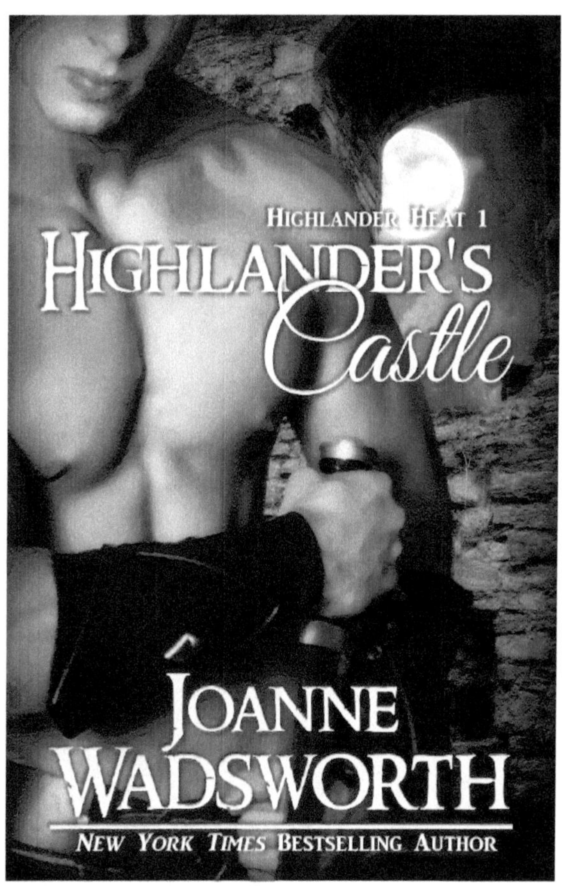

Princesses of Myth

Protector, Book One
Warrior, Book Two
Hunter (Short Story - Included in Warrior, Book Two)
Enchanter, Book Three
Healer, Book Four
Chaser, Book Five

Billionaire Bodyguards

Billionaire Bodyguard Attraction, Book One
Billionaire Bodyguard Boss, Book Two
Billionaire Bodyguard Fling, Book Three

JOANNE WADSWORTH

Joanne Wadsworth is a *New York Times* and *USA Today* Bestselling Author who adores getting lost in the world of romance, no matter what era in time that might be. Hot alpha Highlanders hound her, demanding their stories are told and she's devoted to ensuring they meet their match, whether that be with a feisty lass from the present or far in the past.

Living on a tiny island at the bottom of the world, she calls New Zealand home. Big-dreamer, hoarder of chocolate, and addicted to juicy watermelons since the age of five, she chases after her four energetic children and has her own hunky hubby on the side.

So come and join in all the fun, because this kiwi girl promises to give you her "Hot-Highlander" oath, to bring you a heart-pounding, sexy adventure from the moment you turn the first page. This is where romance meets fantasy and adventure…

To learn more about Joanne and her works, visit
http://www.joannewadsworth.com

www.ingramcontent.com/pod-product-compliance
Lightning Source LLC
Chambersburg PA
CBHW051224210726
48290CB00003B/792